Mating Season

Morgan Clan Bears
Book 1

By
Theresa Hissong

Cover Model:
Nathan Hunt

Cover Photographer:
Christ Monasco
w/
Photography by Christ Monasco

Cover Design:
Custom eBook Covers

Editing by:
Heidi Ryan
Amour the Line Editing

Formatted by:
Wayne Hissong

Other Books by Theresa Hissong:

Fatal Cross Live!
Fatal Desires
Fatal Temptations
Fatal Seduction

Rise of the Pride:
Talon
Winter
Savage
The Birth of an Alpha
Ranger
Kye
The Healer

Standalone Novella:
Something Wicked

Book for Charity:
Fully Loaded

Bad Girls of Romance:
The Huntress

Standalone Erotic Romance:
Rocked (A Rockstar Reverse Harem Novel)

Dedication:

To the bear man, Nathan Hunt.

Contents:

Acknowledgments:

Holy hell!

Where do I start?

Nathan Hunt,

I appreciate you and your friendship more than you know. I have had more fun with this and still laugh at some of the shenanigans your crew has been up to since we started.

#natingseason #thebearstatue #tourbadges

For the readers,

The idea for this book was brought on after seeing Nathan's band, *Shaman's Harvest*, play in Clarksville, TN. There was some drinking involved after the show, I threatened to write him into a book, and that's where it all began.

Nate had no idea what he was getting himself into. Ha!

It took some time, and a few appearances of his character in the Rise of the Pride series for me to convince him to do the cover. It was only fitting he be Drake in visual form....*Right?*

Please remember that the character within came from my own imagination. Yes, Drake is a slow talking bear who wears spurs with his boots, but the rest all made up. Wait, Nate isn't a bear either. I mean, maybe? Wouldn't that be cool if he shifted at night to hunt prey in the woods after a show? Okay, I'll stop now.

I hope you all enjoy this little story.

Rex's book will be next.

Thank you,

Theresa

Chapter 1

The soft breeze across the old farm land owned by the Morgan clan signaled the coming of a new season. Drake Morgan raised his nose to the air, and the bear inside him rumbled from the need that ached deep in his bones. It was a need to prepare his home, his life, for things to come.

Winter had been brutal. He and his brothers had spent most of the time inside, staying warm and sleeping through the worst of the snow and ice. When they had emerged from their hibernation three weeks ago, their first line of business was to prepare their land for the crops. Since it was mid-March, it was time to get the seeds in the ground.

"Spring's comin'," Gunner, Drake's baby brother, drawled as he kicked at the patch of bright green grass next to the gravel driveway. He adjusted the worn baseball hat on his head and wiped his hand over his face in frustration.

"Yup," Drake replied, tossing several limbs into the bed of his truck before running his hand through his curly brown hair. He growled when his fingers caught in the tangled ends, reminding him how his mother used to fuss at him for working with his hair down. She'd known from firsthand experience how frustrating it was to have a headful of corkscrew hair that had a mind of its own.

Gunner and Drake looked more like their mother, while Rex, the middle brother, was the spitting image of their father with his long, dark blond hair. Bears kept their human hair long as it appealed to the opposite sex when it came to searching for mates.

"I hope this year is different." Gunner shook his head and looked up toward the house with a sigh.

It was the same way every year. Their bears called to them to start preparing for the mating season, and that included sprucing up their home. Neither Drake nor his two brothers had found their mates, and this year would probably be no different. They kept to themselves, as far away from the city as possible. It was in their nature not to be around people, finding humans to be the worst companions of all, and it didn't look like there were any female bears in the area again this year. Maybe they needed to travel to a different clan? The thought gave Drake a hard shiver of disgust. He just didn't want to leave his land other than to grab what he needed from town. Going to another town? Not happening.

"I need to go into town for supplies," Drake grunted, ignoring his brother's statement. There was no ranking in their world. Unlike other shifters, bears did whatever the hell they wanted to do and didn't care much for powerful leaders. Drake was in charge of their business only, and he preferred it that way.

"Can you pick up some parts for the tractor?" Rex asked as he approached, wiping his oily hands on an old rag. Rex was the middle brother of the Morgan clan and usually spent his days tinkering around with the equipment they used to care for their land.

"Write down what you need," Drake replied, tossing more branches into his truck. With all of the snow and ice from the winter storms, the trees that dotted their yard had lost several limbs from the weight. Now that the temperatures were warming up, it was time to clean up.

"Corn needs to start being planted next weekend," Gunner worried. "Are you going to have that plow ready?"

"I've never missed a plant date yet, have I?" Rex rolled his eyes and walked away, tucking the dirty rag in his back pocket. His hair was pulled up and away from his face. Grease from the tractor streaked across his left cheek, and his dark-brown eyes looked tired.

"Damn, he's grumpy," Gunner mumbled, walking over to grab some more limbs. He tossed them on top of the ones Drake had gathered and finally looked up at his oldest brother when he grunted in frustration.

"We're all grumpy," Drake snarled. "It's mating season and we have no mates."

"Don't remind me." Gunner flinched and removed his gloves, tucking them in his back pocket. "My bear and his cock are going crazy."

"Your cock is always going crazy," Drake teased with a straight face.

"Yeah, well," Gunner shrugged, "I need a woman."

"Don't we all," Drake mumbled.

"I'm going in to make dinner," Gunner announced. "After that, I'll burn those limbs."

"Get to work," Drake ordered, but it was met by Gunner's two middle fingers raised to his brother.

"Man, fuck off," he barked, stomping off toward the house. He was mumbling something about how he didn't need a female and disappeared inside.

Drake chuckled and dug the keys out of his pocket before climbing into the front seat of his old truck. Rex waved him down as he passed by the barn, handing off a sheet of paper with the required parts written down in his elegant handwriting. Drake never understood why his middle brother preferred working with the machinery when he was smarter than anyone else in the family and could've taken over the business side of the farm.

He stopped at the firepit between the house and the barn to unload the limbs to burn later. With a heavy sigh, Drake turned the truck around and left his sacred land. The drive into town took almost half an hour, and with every mile, he dreaded the task. Drake didn't care to waste time getting his parts and needed supplies, and he usually ignored the stares of the humans who watched him with keen eyes.

Their kind was still unknown. It was the panthers who'd been outed to the humans a few years prior. Riots and protests had broken out, hate groups had been formed, and the U.S. government had stepped in to protect any and all shifters. Not that they wanted, or needed, their help. Being an outcast seemed to be working for them so far, and he had enough strength and gun power to make sure no one came for them this far away from the town. At least, that was the hope he and his brothers shared.

A hate group had kidnapped several species of shifters and took them to a lab off the coast of Maine, but thankfully, the grizzly bears were not included. Drake shook his head. Those damn cats were working with the local law officials to make sure it didn't happen again, and if he found his mate this spring, he was going to make sure no one stepped on his land that didn't belong.

He'd never let his secret out, preferring to stay to his farmland far away from civilization. Being in the most rural of areas in Northern Mississippi, the Morgan clan spent three quarters of the year working from sun up to sun down to grow and harvest their crops. The money they made from selling their corn was set aside for their retirement and to shower their mates with whatever their hearts desired.

As a grizzly bear, their kind were very protective and tended to spoil their females. In their eyes, their mates were everything. They were revered in their society as if they were royalty. The males prepared their den for winter hibernation, making their homes comfortable and safe for their mates. When spring came, and if they were carrying a cub, the male's instincts would go into overdrive and demand they provide for their females for the duration of their pregnancy. It was a pull that couldn't be denied.

Drake passed the werepanther-owned bar, *The Deuce*, and made a mental note to stop in for a beer and check on those cats. They'd become somewhat of an ally to his clan. He didn't trust anyone to begin with, human or shifter, but Talon Shaw and his pride had proven their worth when they'd saved his bear clan from exposure to the humans a few years back. His brother, Gunner, had been taken by a group of scientists who were gathering up shifters and then left him for dead in the county dump. Thankfully, he'd gotten away, but not before the law had seen video of him shifting.

Good thing for the shifters, the sheriff of the

town wasn't quite human himself. Sheriff Lynch was some sort of angel, and he had been tasked with watching over the cats. Drake hoped the sheriff stayed far away, because he didn't need anyone protecting them. He was taking care of that on his own.

The bell over the door to the parts store clanged as he entered ten minutes before they closed. Tulley McCray was sitting at the counter with his cowboy hat pulled low over his eyes. Drake went on about gathering his supplies, making a stack by the register. Tulley nodded and retuned to flipping through the local paper. Drake made note of the headline and huffed quietly. The humans were still talking about the raids on the labs that had studied the shifters. Thankfully, he didn't have anything to do with that, and his family was safe from being known to the humans.

"Ready for the spring?" Tulley asked as he ambled to his feet, taking a moment to stretch.

"Getting things prepped," Drake answered, grabbing one last thing before removing the piece of paper from his pocket. "Need some parts for the plow."

"Let me see that list Rex gave you," Tulley chuckled. The older man had been selling parts to them for years and knew how Drake's brother worked. "Ah, I have one of these, but the other two I have to order and can have them delivered to you day after tomorrow."

"That's fine," Drake grumbled, not really wanting to have anyone deliver anything to his home, but it would be better that he not make two trips into town that week. He had more important things to do.

"Let's get you rung up," Tulley said as he keyed in the items on the register.

Drake swiped his credit card and took the receipt. The parts were costly, but it was what they needed. He didn't put up a fuss because the business had been lucrative and they were doing quite well for themselves. Tulley shook Drake's hand with a promise to send someone out to their land as soon as possible.

As he turned to leave, a sweet scent crossed his nose, stopping Drake in his tracks. It was honeysuckle, but more powerful. His heart galloped in his chest and his cock stirred to life. His face turned blood red from the blush of embarrassment.

"Did you forget something?" Tulley asked as he walked up behind the bear.

"What's that scent?" Drake growled, feeling a strange anger inside him at the human male who had approached him from behind. It took all he had to push his bear down to keep from unleashing his claws and taking a swipe at him.

"I don't know what you're talking about."

Tulley frowned, taking a deep breath.

"Honeysuckle," Drake mumbled as he regained control over himself. His long curls brushed over his shoulder as he turned to look around the store. There were no candles or frilly, feminine concoctions in sight. *What the hell is wrong with me?*

"No," Tulley said as he shook his head. "I don't have any of that in my store."

"Sorry," Drake replied, shaking his head and turning for the door.

He really needed to get back to his land. Being around humans was driving him insane.

A blonde female pushed the door open as he was about to grab the handle. She was beautiful for a human, and he'd be a fool not to have noticed. Her hair was so blonde it looked like it'd been kissed by the sun. She was half a foot shorter than him, and her curves were what shifter men dreamed of when they thought of their mates. He shouldn't be eyeing a human female, but this one intrigued him.

"I'm sorry, Tulley. I forgot this in my car." The female handed Tulley a bag and flipped her keys around on her index finger as if she were nervous.

"No worries, Tessa." The old, human male smiled and took the bag from her. She waved and turned to exit, freezing when she saw Drake still standing in the doorway. Her sapphire-blue eyes widened, and she took a step back. Drake didn't fault her. He was a predator, and even though no one knew he was, it was in a human's nature to be wary of someone his size.

"Excuse me," she mumbled as she ducked her head and passed him to leave the building. As soon as she was out the door, he inhaled deep and cleared his throat when his chest rumbled from the scent of honeysuckle. She was the source, and if she were of his kind, Drake would've followed her out to talk to her. The fact that she was human kept him from doing just that.

Drake frowned as she attempted to crank her car. He could see her mouth moving as if she were cursing, and a small smirk tugged at the corner of his lip. The engine fired up after a few tries, and the woman was on her way.

"Need anything else, Drake?" Tulley called out.

"Naw, I'm good," he drawled and headed toward his truck. He'd had enough of humans for the day, and it was time to return to his home where he could have some peace and quiet

Chapter 2

Tessa Ward gathered the package to deliver to the Morgan farm. Her boss, Tulley, insisted it be taken immediately. She rolled her eyes as she pulled her keys from the back pocket of her jeans. This guy must be one hell of a customer for her boss to offer her double time pay for the hour and a half it'd take her to head south of town and return to the store.

Whatever he wants. I could use the money.

She blew out a harsh breath as she walked out of the building. It'd been several days since she'd had a day off, and her feet were killing her. When the bills came due, you had to have the money to pay them. Thankfully, she'd found this new job with Tulley a month ago. It'd been a learning experience, and he was very good about working around her schedule at the diner. Working two jobs was a pain in the ass, but it kept the lights on. It wasn't like she had any friends in town to hang out with anyway. So, working was all she had.

"Wait!" Tulley hollered just as she reached the car. The old man shuffled his way down the sidewalk and held out his hand. Tessa felt the tears welling up in her eyes when she saw what he was holding. "Gas money."

"Tulley," she warned, waving off his offer. "You're already paying me extra to do this."

"Humph," he frowned. "Paychecks don't cut until next week. Take this now, and you can pay me back later." She smiled warmly and accepted his offer of twenty dollars. She knew he wouldn't take it out of her check, but she'd find a way to pay him back.

Stopping at the gas station, she went inside and told the clerk to put fifteen dollars on gas and she bought a small bag of chips and a water with the rest, leaving just over two dollars in her pocket. That snack was going to be her dinner for the night.

Tessa was tired, but she headed down to the Morgan farm south of town as directed by her boss. When she arrived, she checked the address on the mailbox to make sure she was at the right place. The home was hidden by thick trees lining the property. Even with the bare limbs, the house was impossible to see from the road. As she came into a clearing, she smiled at the large home before her. The porch wrapped around the entire log cabin home, and to the left was a huge barn and several pieces of equipment lined up next to its doors. If she could afford to own her own home, this would be the perfect place for her. She could see herself sitting on the covered front porch, sipping coffee on a cool spring morning.

She put the car in park and shook away the

dream. There was no way she'd ever be able to afford a place like that. Instead, she stepped out of her car and walked around to the passenger side, reaching for the box Tulley had given her to deliver. When she turned around and closed the door with a bump from her hip, three very large men were standing on the steps leading up to the front door.

"What are you doing here?" the bigger of the three bellowed. He was the one who had been at the store the other day. She'd been in such a hurry, she hadn't really paid much attention to him. But now? Now, she saw him. He was large, his shoulders wide. His long, corkscrew hair fell forward to cover most of his face as he headed down the stairs off the old porch. There was a wildness about the man, but she steeled her spine and held her head high.

"Tulley sent me," she offered, holding up the box. She'd been bullied for years, and she wasn't going to take it from this man, either. "You could be a little nicer, you know."

"Don't like people on my land who don't belong," he called out, narrowing his dark-brown eyes as he walked toward her.

"Are you Mr. Morgan?" she asked, looking over his shoulder at the other two men. Both of them stepped off the porch and walked closer, only stopping a few feet away.

The one with the dark-blond hair tucked a rag

in his back pocket and shook his head before walking away. The second, and younger looking one, folded his arms over his chest and tucked his chin to hide his eyes behind the baseball cap he was wearing. Tessa couldn't quite make out his features, but that wasn't why she was there. She had to make a delivery, and from the scowl on this man's face, she needed to drop it and get out of there quickly.

"I'm Drake Morgan," he grunted, but the sound of his slow drawl sent a shiver down her spine. "And you are?"

"Tessa." She cleared her throat. "Tessa Ward, and I work for Tulley."

"I remember," he growled. Tessa's eyes widened, but she quickly righted her features when she realized she probably looked foolish. All she wanted to do was drop off the part and leave this man's land. He obviously didn't want her there anymore than she wanted to be there.

"Anyhow," she smirked, "here is one of your parts. Tulley wanted me to let you know the other part will be another two days. Someone will deliver it to you." That someone wouldn't be her.

"He told me the parts would be in today," Drake retorted, his eyebrows pushing together in frustration. "I need that part, little one."

"I'm sorry," she shrugged, ignoring his endearment. "If they come in sooner, I'm sure Tulley will deliver them himself."

"I want you to deliver them," he ordered as his chest swelled with a deep inhale. And yes, that deep growl of a sentence he'd strung together was, in fact, an order. "Now, set the box down and be on your way."

"Yes, sir," she replied, making sure she didn't roll her eyes or kick dirt on his boots. Geez, he was super bossy and grumpy.

As she bent over, Tessa heard him inhale long and deep again. She didn't even look at him to see what he was doing. As of that moment, she wanted nothing more than to go to her tiny apartment and go to sleep.

"Honeysuckle?" he asked, shocking Tessa for a moment. She stood up and looked him in the eyes. Drake blinked several times and gritted his teeth. She didn't know if she should answer him or run.

"What?" she asked with a frown.

"Your scent," he whispered in awe and took a step closer. "It's honeysuckle."

"Uh, no," she shook her head, "I'm not wearing anything."

"Forgive me." He paused, taking a moment to clear his throat and step away. Tessa watched as he scratched at his short beard, sliding his hand around the back of his neck to work out the tension there.

"Be here tomorrow with my part," Drake

ordered after a sudden shift in his mood.

"But Tulley said it may be Friday," she began, but a hard glare from Mr. Morgan shut her right up.

"Tomorrow," he barked, and walked over to open the door to her car. Tessa didn't waste time and slid into the seat, praying the car would crank on the first try. When it did, she pulled the door and slammed it shut, putting the car in reverse and leaving the Morgan's land as fast as she could.

When she looked in the rearview mirror, Drake was rooted to the same spot, watching her as she drove away. A shiver raced up her spine as he faded from sight. Tulley never told her Drake Morgan was handsome, or that he was an asshole.

Chapter 3

Drake walked into the barn and set the box the human female had delivered down on the table Rex used to work on parts for the farm equipment. He heard a curse from under the plow his brother was working on and walked over to offer assistance.

"Only one part showed up today," Drake announced. "Hope you can work on that one until the other one is delivered tomorrow."

"Humph, guess that's two days in a row a human comes on our land," Rex growled as he dropped his tool on the ground.

"Believe me," Drake rolled his eyes even though Rex couldn't see him, "I don't want anyone else on our land."

"But the human female was a looker," Rex admitted as he emerged from the underbelly of the plow. He wiped his hands on the old rag he kept in his back pocket and walked over to the table.

"I didn't notice," Drake lied. He had noticed how stunning she was, and the scent of honeysuckle piqued his interest more than it should. His bear rumbled in his mind as a form of agreement with his thoughts.

"I can scent your lie." Rex narrowed his eyes. "Does your bear like her?"

"No," he lied, again.

"So, that's a yes." Rex paused. His brother shook his head and a small smile curved his full lips. "She can be changed into one of us."

"No," Drake barked. "She's a human."

"She's a beautiful human," Gunner announced as he entered the barn. Drake growled low in his throat as the youngest Morgan approached. His bear didn't want his brothers talking to, or even looking at, Tessa.

"She's not mine," Drake stated.

"She could be if you touched her," Rex shrugged. "Maybe when…"

"Enough!" Drake snarled. His brothers were going to drive him insane this mating season, just like they'd done every other spring for as long as he could remember. "I will not touch a human, ever. This isn't up for discussion."

"Maybe I'll touch her then," Gunner teased, but sucked in his breath when Drake's hand wrapped around the youngest brother's throat. Drake's fangs broke through his gums so quickly, the coppery taste of his own blood was thick on his human tongue. "K…kidding."

"No one touches that female," Drake warned, giving Gunner a good shake before letting him go.

Fuck! What the hell was wrong with him? He shouldn't feel protective of a human female. They were the enemy, and the last thing he ever wanted was to have one for a mate.

"Sure," Rex said in an unamused tone. His middle brother grabbed the part Tessa had delivered and went back to work as if Drake choking out his brother was an everyday occurrence.

Sometimes, it was.

Drake left the barn and headed toward his home. Every step he took, his bear prowled in his mind, thinking of the blonde human and how her hips swayed and her long hair bounced as she walked. His cock ached from the images of her that flashed through his mind. The wide, blue eyes of her stare when she was frightened and the soft sigh she produced when he ordered her to put the box on the ground just made it worse.

He needed a cold beer and an even colder shower.

He had to keep telling himself, and his bear, that she was human and the scent of honeysuckle was probably what made his bear so interested in her. It had nothing to do with how beautiful she was, or the fact that her body was perfect for his human side.

Nope, not at all.

Tessa lifted the large tray of food from the kitchen window at the diner and headed toward the table by the front door. The family of five thanked her and dug into their food. The mother reminded Tessa of her own mother as she doted over her children and smiled warmly at their father. A pain bloomed in her chest when she thought of how much she missed her own family, but knew it was better to keep her distance until her life calmed down.

Shaking those thoughts from her mind, Tessa tucked the empty tray under her arm and walked toward the kitchen. There was no need to darken her day with thoughts of things she couldn't control. She had work to do.

Gaia, her boss, was filling the coffee machine to brew a new pot and almost every table in the place was full. As she looked around the small room, she was fine with it being busy, because the tips she'd receive during her morning shift would hopefully pay for the grocery trip she'd planned on her day off.

"Tessa, could you be a dear and bring Mr. Brown some butter?" Gaia asked as she passed with a platter of food to deliver to her tables. Her boss was in her mid-forties and beautiful. Her long, black hair fell to her waist, but when she was at the diner, Gaia kept it up in a bun at the back of her head.

"Sure." She nodded and hurried over to the elderly man's table.

The bell over the door jingled with the arrival of a new customer. The cool morning air crossed over her skin, causing goosebumps to raise on her arms. When Tessa looked up, she noticed the sheriff enter and head for a barstool at the counter after making a quick sweep of the diner with his keen eyes.

This was the third time he'd been in since she had started at the diner. The lawman had an air of authority about him that made people take notice. The customers looked up from their meals and some straightened their backs as he walked toward the counter where there were two empty stools for those eating alone. Gaia nodded for Tessa to take his order since she was held up with her table. Tessa tried to calm her nerves as she approached him with a menu and cup of coffee.

"Morning, Sheriff."

"Morning, Tessa." Sheriff Lynch smiled and took the menu from her hand. "How are you today?"

"So far, so good," she shrugged. "Do you know what you'd like to order, or do you need another moment?"

"Give me a few minutes," he replied, flipping

over the menu. She nodded and went about cleaning a table just vacated by two men who worked for the water company. She used a rag to wipe it down and added a clean set of silverware at each place setting.

A look at the clock over her shoulder showed it was nearing nine, and thankfully, the breakfast crowd would dwindle a little so she could take a break and get off her feet for a few minutes after she served the sheriff. She'd already helped Tony, the cook, prep for the morning rush at five that morning, and she was probably going to need a cup or two of coffee during her break.

"Just give me the breakfast special," Sheriff Lynch ordered. "I'll take another cup of coffee when you come back around with the food."

"Sounds great." She smiled and wrote down his order on the pad in her pocket. "It'll be out shortly."

As she helped the other customers, Tessa noticed the sheriff kept looking at her from the corner of his eye. Gaia stopped and spoke to him softly. She felt a moment of panic set in, wondering why he was so observant of her. Had she done something wrong? No, it couldn't be. Tessa had never even gotten a speeding ticket.

"Is there anything else I can get for you?" she asked as she cleared away his plate.

"How are you liking our little town?" he inquired, setting his napkin on the counter. Tessa scooped it up along with his cup and balanced it on the plate in her hands. She noticed her hands were shaking and she quickly tightened her hold on the dishes.

"It's very nice," she said, clearing her throat. "What I've seen of it, that is."

"You're working for Tulley, too?" he asked, swiveling the barstool so he could face her. She took a small step back and nodded instead of giving a verbal reply. She would probably answer him with a shaky voice otherwise. "Where did you say you were from?"

"I didn't," she whispered as her heart began to race. Why was he asking her so many questions?

"Okay, understood," he relented after a small pause. Sheriff Lynch stood and pulled out his wallet, dropping some cash on the counter. He gave her a smile and left without any further questions. As soon as he was gone, she hurried to the kitchen to drop off the dishes, making an excuse to use the restroom. When she closed and locked the door, Tessa leaned against the bathroom counter and let out a harsh breath.

"I don't want to be found."

She waited for a few minutes before returning to the kitchen. Tony was just setting an order in the window, and Gaia was wiping her hands at the sink. "Everything okay, Tessa?"

"Oh, yes," she lied, grabbing a large tray to carry the food. She hurried along and served the last of the morning rush.

It took another thirty minutes for the place to slow down enough for Tessa to take a break. Gaia hurried her along to the small breakroom in the back with a cup of coffee in hand.

She removed her phone and did an internet search for her ex, hoping she'd read something on him being in jail where he couldn't come and find her again. To her dismay, there was nothing new online.

Why was the sheriff being so nosey?

Tessa wanted nothing more than to be left alone so she could go on with her life. She thought back to Drake Morgan and his need for peace on his land. She wanted that more than anything and would make it her life's goal to find a little place in the country like his.

Chapter 4

It was five minutes before the start of her shift at the parts store when Tessa arrived. Tulley sat on a stool behind the counter, reading the local newspaper. The old man frowned as she rushed around, dropping her bag in the bottom drawer of his desk.

"You okay?" Tulley asked aloud, folding the paper and setting it on the desk. Her boss looked worried, but she waved away his concern with a flutter of her fingers.

"I'm fine, just running late," she huffed and sat heavily in the chair. "The diner was busy and I was late leaving."

"Did you eat lunch today at all?" he worried.

"A banana," she replied. "Gaia sent me off with a bowl of chicken pasta for my dinner. It's in my bag."

"Gaia is a good woman," he said with a smile, causing Tessa to feel a blush paint her cheeks at the way his face brightened when talking about the lady who owned the diner.

"Do you have the part for Mr. Morgan?" she asked, changing the subject.

"I sure do, but Drake called and asked if you

could bring it later today." He nodded and pointed to the box at the end of the counter. "It's heavy. I'll load it in your car before you leave."

"What do you need me to work on today?"

"We had a shipment arrive earlier, and it needs to be entered into the computer," he said, ruffling through a stack of papers. He pulled three from the stack and handed them over. "I've already counted the parts and the paperwork matches up."

"I'll take care of this right now," she offered, and took a seat behind the desk. As she updated the inventory, Tessa watched the clock, wondering why Drake Morgan wanted her to wait to come to his home. The thought of going out there later in the day gave her pause, but she knew Tulley wouldn't send her anywhere that could be dangerous, no matter how much of an asshole the customer was to her.

"When you're done, you can take the part to the Morgan's farm," he explained. "Let me have your keys and I'll put the box in your trunk." She handed over the keys and left her boss to take the part to her car.

She'd become very fond of Tulley. He was always watching out for her, and she appreciated it. Having him there made being alone in a new city a little more bearable. The old man treated her like a daughter, and she felt more at ease at the parts store than anywhere else.

Movement outside made her look up from her work. Tulley was standing in the parking lot talking to one of the local deputies. His hands were tucked in his blue dress pants, and when he laughed, the wrinkles around his mouth deepened when he smiled.

The phone rang, but she didn't take her eyes off the deputy as she took the call from another farmer in the area looking for his own parts. Tessa knew she was being paranoid since the sheriff had come into the diner that morning.

She couldn't worry about her past. She'd left her last home in a hurry, and there was nothing tying her to Olive Branch. If her ex wanted to find her, she was sure he'd do it. Her only hope was that he would give up trying to get her to come back to him, and if she really analyzed the encounter with the sheriff, Tessa knew his inquiry into her personal information had nothing to do with the man she'd been running from for the last year and a half. He wouldn't let her be found, would he? Maybe she should've talked to him…to Tulley…hell, even Gaia.

"You ready to head to the Morgan's farm?" Tulley asked as he entered the building. Tessa typed the final numbers into the computer and initialed the corner of the packing slip, filing it away in the drawer above where she kept her purse.

"I'm ready," she said, then hesitated, biting her lip as she gathered her things. Tulley poured himself a cup of coffee even though it was nearing dinner time.

"Is everything okay?" Tulley asked. "You've been on edge since you arrived."

"What do you know about Drake Morgan?" she blurted, instantly regretting her question when Tulley narrowed his green eyes at her.

"He's an honest and fair man." Tulley defended the farmer. "His family has been the largest producer of corn in our community for generations."

"Okay," she blushed, feeling bad about her worry about the man. Maybe Drake just didn't like her? "He seemed a little angry when I disturbed him with the last delivery. Are you sure he knows I'm coming tonight?"

"I talked to him personally this morning," Tulley promised. "Why? Did he say anything to upset you?"

"No, not really," she scowled. "Maybe he was just in a bad mood because we didn't have all of his parts."

"Well, you don't worry about Drake Morgan," Tulley huffed. "He can be a bit grumpy, but he's nothing but a big ole teddy bear."

"Okay, sure," she mumbled and removed her keys from her purse. "I'll see you on Monday."

"Have a good day off Sunday," he said with a smile, changing the subject of the handsome farmer.

"I plan on it," she replied, and left the store. It

was Thursday, and she only had the morning shift at the diner the next two mornings. Saturday afternoon through Monday morning was her only time off. Thirty-six hours to rest, do laundry, and go to the store was all the time she had to herself during the week.

As she drove, she imagined a day when she could work a normal nine to five job and have the weekends off. If she ever made friends, she could have a normal life again. She couldn't even remember the last time she went out to have a beer.

The drive to the Morgan farm took about thirty minutes from the town square where the parts store was located. Tessa leaned over the steering wheel and looked up at the still-barren trees. They'd soon start filling up with leaves again as the temperatures warmed with each passing day. She was happy to have a bit of warmth back into her life. The winter had been too much for her. While she loved the beauty of a freshly fallen snow, working in the mess made it unbearable.

Tessa turned onto the road leading to Drake's home, and she squared her shoulders. She wouldn't let that man intimidate her again, but she still hoped she could give him the parts with no problems this time.

As she pulled into his driveway and passed through the grove of trees that lined the property leading to where his house stood, she sighed heavily when she noticed all three of the Morgan men standing on their wrap around porch. One of them was holding a shotgun, but set it down as soon as her car came into view. That had to be a good thing, right?

From the last encounter, Tessa knew they were apprehensive about people they didn't know coming on their land. As far out in the country they lived, she guessed anyone who came onto their land would've been a friend. She felt sorry for anyone who stumbled upon this home with malicious intent on their mind. Drake alone could scare away the hardest of thieves. Now that she knew they carried weapons, she'd make sure she was in and out of there as soon as humanly possible.

She quickly pulled her long, blonde hair up into a ponytail and turned off the car, jumping out as Drake ambled down the stairs from his perch by the front door. "I'm here to drop off your part, then I will be on my way."

She wanted to make sure he knew she wasn't going to stay. As much as she loved his land and log cabin-style home, she knew she wasn't welcomed.

The box was heavy as she lifted it from her trunk with a soft grunt. Drake's eyebrows pushed forward and he took a step toward her but paused.

"Put the box down," he ordered, pointing to the

ground at her feet. She refrained from rolling her eyes, but she didn't silence the huff of frustration that rolled from her lips. He'd made her do the same thing the last time she'd been at his house. Why did he do that?

"Umm, okay," she replied, and bent over at the waist to set the box down.

Yes, she was probably really stupid. Tessa found Drake very good looking, and even though she'd sworn off dating ever again, she would totally flirt with him if he wasn't such a jerk. This was the second time he'd grunted at her when he talked.

Screw this. Put the box down and go home, Tessa.

Tessa knew she was in trouble the moment she realized the box was too heavy and her body lurched forward. Her boot caught the back of her other foot as she stumbled to evenly distribute her weight and she fell toward Drake, but she didn't hit the ground.

Large hands wrapped around her arms and the scent of the forest reached her nose, but something was…off. Drake Morgan's touch sent her body into a hormone induced frenzy. When she looked up into his eyes, they'd changed color…to a bright, glowing gold.

"Oh, my…" she breathed out as he held her close, but she frowned when she saw his mouth open wide, revealing large fangs where his human teeth should've been. She tamped down the need to rub herself against him and just stared at his mouth.

"You're my mate," he snarled. Drake's voice echoed off the trees as the other two men came down the steps to stare at her in awe. "You're human, and you're my mate."

Tessa gasped, her hand covering her mouth. She didn't know he was a shifter. What was he? Was he like the others in town? Oh my god, was he a panther shifter?

"I'm no one's," she argued, shaking her head.

"That's where you're wrong." Drake stepped back to look her over. "You are mine, Tessa…all mine."

"Are you…are you a…panther?" she asked, but her eyes widened when he bared his fangs at her. Drake felt bad for scaring her, but she needed to understand he was no panther. He was a bear, and bears were the strongest shifters out there as far as he was concerned. "I know about shifters, Drake. Don't lie to me."

"I am not," he snapped. How dare she think he

was like those Shaw cats. "Those panthers are nothing like me."

"What are you?" she asked. Drake could see the wonder and questions in her eyes as she reached up to touch his face. Her touch was like an angel itself was consoling him, and his bear bucked inside when it scented honeysuckle on her skin. He had the sudden urge to taste her. "Your eyes…"

"Fuck," he growled, turning his head so she couldn't see his eyes.

"Don't hide from me," she whispered, turning his face when he started to look away. "I'm not oblivious, Drake. I know you are some sort of shifter. What are you?"

"My beast is present," Drake admitted, unsure of how much he should tell his human mate. Was she going to out him to the humans? Would she run away from him?

"Beast?" she gasped and jerked away. "What type of beast are you?"

"Drake?" Rex called out as he approached. Drake growled low in his throat at another male coming toward his mate. She wasn't marked by him, and that alone set his bear on edge. "What's going on? Is she your mate?"

"That's close enough," Drake warned, holding his hand out to stop his brother.

"*Is she your mate*?" Gunner repeated Rex's

question, but his voice was laced with a sliver of hope.

"Mate? Why do you keep calling me that?" Tessa asked, narrowing her eyes on Drake. She placed her hands on her hips and waited for him to answer. She had sass, and he liked it.

"He's a bear shifter. And when he touched you, his beast claimed you for his own," Gunner, the youngest, yelled. Drake turned slowly, his eyes flashing gold as he watched his brother shrug. "I did it for you since you wouldn't tell her."

"A bear?" she chuckled, making Drake turn his head back in her direction. "Really?"

"Yes, really," he replied, gritting his teeth. The cat was out of the bag, so to speak, so he was left with being honest with her, hoping she wouldn't tell the other humans. "We are all bears, and this is our den. Humans aren't allowed here, but apparently, you're my mate. Our nature tells us when we touch the one we are destined to be with for eternity." If she knew how they mated, she'd probably deny him and run away screaming…maybe even run to the police.

"I don't think so," she scoffed, shaking her head. "Did that once…never happening again."

"You had a mate?" Drake asked. His beast was clawing at his skin to be set free. The bear inside him wanted to show her the shift. He wanted Tessa to forget all about her other mate.

"Well, a husband," she frowned. "I divorced him and ran far away from him. That's why I'm here in Olive Branch."

"You're hiding from your human?" Gunner asked with a frown.

"He's not my human anymore." She sighed dramatically. "Look, I didn't mean to come on your land again and upset you, and I won't tell anyone about you being a shifter, because it is none of my business. I need to be going."

"Why are you hiding from this human?" Drake growled, his eyes focused on her face. He needed to know more.

"Ahh, I really don't want to talk to you about this," she said, taking a step away. Drake's head tilted to the side when he heard her stomach rumble.

"You're hungry," he grunted. "I'll feed you before you leave. Come inside."

"Wow, you like telling me what to do, huh?"

"I do, and you will listen," he ordered, holding out his hand for the female to go ahead of him and enter the house. His two brothers turned and walked away first. Rex was the first one to reach the door, waiting for Drake and Tessa to follow. Gunner disappeared inside.

"You're a stranger to me," she scoffed. "I'm not going inside that house."

"Tulley can assure you I am not a threat to a

female," Drake said, dropping his hand to his side. He reached into his back pocket and removed his phone, offering it to her. "You can call him if you'd like."

Tessa stared at the phone and raised her eyes to Drake. It was obvious she had trust issues as well. He stepped back when Tessa pushed away his phone. "Tulley already assured me you were an honest and fair man."

"I've known Tulley for many years," Drake explained. "Won't you join us for dinner?"

"I will stay for dinner, but then I must be going," she resigned, crossing her arms.

"Thank you," Drake said, holding out his hand for her to go first up the stairs to the porch.

The little hitch of breath she released when she walked inside made Drake's chest swell with pride. His home was made for his and his brothers' mates. The log cabin was much more grandiose inside with a large kitchen and living room. There were three hallways off the living room, and beyond those were each brother's rooms. The hallways had their own exits, but the rest of the bedrooms were hidden in the ground behind the main home for protection and the winter months when it was time to hibernate.

"This is beautiful," she sighed, placing her hand on her chest. She paused and inhaled deep, "What's that smell?"

"Beef stew," Drake said after clearing his

throat. She was his mate, and if she didn't like it, he'd toss it out and make something she'd enjoy. "Do you not like it?"

"I'm not picky." She frowned, and Drake felt the sadness rolling off of her. "I'll eat anything."

"What's wrong?" he growled, immediately on the defensive.

"I haven't had a home cooked meal in a very long time," she admitted.

"Do you not cook?" he questioned as he brothers started filling bowls from the huge pot on the stove.

"I can, but since I work two jobs, I don't have time for more than what I can grab at the diner during my shift, and when I get home for the night, I just want to rest." She paused to shake her head as if she was expelling a bad memory. "I appreciate your hospitality, but after I eat, I must go."

She was his mate. There was no way he could let her go now. She needed to be marked so no other male would come around her.

"Promise me you'll let me show you something before you leave?" he asked, but his eyes were pleading with the female.

"I guess," she shrugged.

"Come eat," he said, without so much demand that time.

"See, you can be nice," she teased and took a

seat at the kitchen table. Drake took a bowl from Rex and set it in front of Tessa with a spoon.

"I can be," he winked. "What would you like to drink?"

"Water is fine," she blushed. Drake froze behind her when he returned from getting her a glass of water. The sight of his mate sitting there with her back straight, hands on her lap, sent a thrill through his veins. Long blonde hair cascaded down her back in waves, touching her waist. She was full of sass, but something about her posture told him she was a bit submissive.

"You may eat," he whispered as he touched her shoulder. He felt a small shiver roll through her body, and he knew she felt the power of their connection too. She nodded, picked up the spoon that rested next to the bowl, and took her first bite. Drake's cock hardened when she moaned aloud.

"This is delicious," she gushed, taking two more bites before looking up at him. Her big blue eyes were glassy as if she were about to cry. "Thank you."

"What's wrong?" he growled, dropping to his knees next to her.

"I'm sorry." Tessa waved her hand in front of her face to dry the tears. "I don't know why I'm so emotional. Please forgive me, I must go."

Tessa began to stand, but Drake put his hand on

her shoulder again, carefully pushing her back down into the seat. "You will eat a full meal before you leave our home. There will be no arguments."

"Um, okay," she stammered, turning back in her seat to continue eating. "Are you going to eat, too?"

"Our females eat first," he admitted, finally taking a seat next to her.

"That's very nice of you," she said, and smiled. "So, is that a bear thing?"

Drake's lip lifted into a smile and her eyes darkened with heat when he laughed. "It is. We cherish our mates."

"And I'm your mate?" she asked, a soft blush painting her cheeks.

"My bear has claimed you," he stated. "We are ruled by the animals that live inside us, and our world is different from the humans. They're ungrateful for the things they have and the people who love them."

"And you don't like humans?" she continued questioning, and took another bite of food. He didn't know what to think of the female. She was docile, but inquisitive. Tessa Ward was beautiful.

"We live a solitary life here, and we don't care for humans to know our secret." He paused to shake his head. Why the fuck was he telling her this?

"Oh, I won't tell a soul," she promised, holding up her hand as if to stop him from speaking. "I understand the need for secrecy, believe me. Plus, having a home like this would be the perfect place to escape. You're so far out from society."

"Do you like my home?" he asked, feeling hopeful he could convince her to stay tonight…and the next.

"It is everything I ever wanted in a home if I was able to build it myself." She sighed as she glanced around the living room. "It's perfect, and you have done an amazing job with it."

Drake's hand latched onto her wrist, and Tessa gasped when he pulled her out of the chair. She didn't struggle as his lips crashed down on hers. This woman was his mate, and he'd do anything to keep her…even if she was a human.

Rex sat in his room, completely jealous of his brother. He'd found his mate just by the woman stepping foot onto their land. How had that even happened? He and Gunner had been going out twice a month to clubs and bars in the area, trying to meet women, but none of them appealed to their bears.

Rex knew he'd never be that damn lucky. No one ever came out to their property unannounced. Drake better treat that female right, or Rex would kick his older brother's ass. They all knew the oldest of the Morgan Clan had never liked humans. Hell, Rex and Gunner understood why, but they didn't share the disgust for them like Drake did.

"Hey, bro," Gunner said after knocking on the door frame. "Want to go to that cat bar and have a beer?"

"Yeah," he said, standing up from his desk. "Do you think this female will make Drake less bitter toward the humans?"

"I really don't know," Gunner sighed. "He may never get over the death of our parents."

Their mother and father were killed eight years ago by a human male who was strung out on human illegal drugs. He'd broken into the office of their farming business early one morning. The male tried to rob them but ended up shooting them point-blank when he realized the business didn't have any cash on site.

Drake, Rex, and Gunner were left the business, barely knowing how to run it successfully. Drake was twenty-eight at the time and ran the machines that harvested the corn crops. He didn't know anything else. Thankfully, the three of them worked hard over the next two seasons to keep the business alive.

Today, they were the largest corn growers in the area.

"Let's give them some space and see what happens," Rex suggested.

"You don't think he will hurt her, do you?" Gunner worried.

"He may hate humans, but he would never hurt a female…no matter her species," Rex answered.

The two of them quietly walked out of the tunnel leading to Rex's room. When they entered the living room, Drake was pulling his mate up from her chair. He cupped her face and kissed her hard. Rex smiled and turned to Gunner. "See, he's going to spoil her."

They slipped out the back door on the other side of the living room and walked around the house to jump in Rex's truck. They'd give Drake some time with his mate. Rex was hopeful he and Gunner would get lucky at the werepanther-owned bar, *The Deuce*.

Tessa gasped and pushed at Drake's chest. He released her as soon as she began to struggle. "What the hell are you doing?"

"You're mine, Tessa," he vowed, taking a step

back. Drake's eyes were bright and his fangs were long in his mouth. "As much as I hate humans, my bear has chosen you."

"Well," she scowled, "I didn't pick you, and why would I when you tell me you hate humans?"

"I need to mate with you," he replied, and made a face as if he were in pain. Tessa looked down and blushed when she noticed an obvious erection through his denim jeans. *Wow! Impressive!* What the hell was wrong with her? This man…this *beast* wanted to claim her for his own? How did that even work? Why was she so turned on by him, and why was she considering it?

"If your idea of mating is what I imagine it to be, there will be none of that today, Mr. Morgan," she said, standing her ground. She barely knew this man, and every interaction she'd had with him over the last few days had been less than acceptable.

"Ms. Ward," he smirked, the corner of his full lips pulling up on one side. She could still see one of his extended fangs, and she shivered from the sight. "You can't leave my land. You must stay here and let me explain things to you."

"Are you holding me hostage?"

"Only if you're into that sort of thing," he shrugged, but betrayed himself when his eyes heated. *Does he like the idea of holding me prisoner?* The thought of playing with him awakened a need inside her…a need she hadn't felt in some time.

"Are you demanding I stay?" Tessa asked, baiting him to see if he was as dominant as she was starting to believe he was. That would explain his sharp commands the first time they'd interacted.

"You have your own free will, but I'd prefer you to stay," he said, offering her a way out.

"I will consider it," she heard herself say. *Holy hell? What is wrong with you, Tessa?* Drake fascinated her. She wanted to know more about him, but not in any way that she'd ever tell the humans about him.

No, this sexy shifter man called to her in a way she'd never felt before. When they touched, she felt something strange. It was a feral need to be protected by him. Her body betrayed her, and the ache she felt between her legs was a dead giveaway of how much he affected her.

"Call Tulley and tell him you delivered the part," he ordered, his eyes heating with his words. "Also, call the diner and tell them you won't be in tomorrow."

"I have to work," she replied. Drake wrapped his hand around the back of her neck again and with his touch, her body relaxed into his hold.

"Maybe I can change your mind," he offered right before his soft lips crashed down on hers.

Tessa felt wetness pool between her legs as

Drake kissed her forcefully. She hadn't had a response to a man like that since she'd first met her ex. Drake was so much different than Bradley. Where her ex was tall with lean muscle, Drake was nothing but bulk and pure strength. She should be afraid of Drake, but something inside her fired to life when he touched her. He was an animal…a shifter. She didn't know much about the paranormal, and she didn't know if he had any powers like what was written about in some of the romance books she'd read.

"Are you making me feel this way?" she whispered when he finally released her lips. Tessa tilted her head to the side and ran her fingers over his soft beard. She never cared much for men with beards, but it worked for Drake.

"I'm not." He shook his head and cupped her face. "Shifters find their forever mates by the first touch. My bear knows you are to be ours, and I don't expect you to understand. There is a lot you don't know about us, but I assure you, I have no power over your thoughts."

"Can…can I see him?" she asked, her voice shaking as she asked. "Can I see the bear?"

"You are very curious, huh?" he grinned.

"Very," she breathed.

Drake inhaled deep, releasing his breath at the tail end of a long sigh. His eyes flashed a golden hue, and he leaned in to bite her bottom lip softly. "You smell delicious."

Tessa couldn't even answer. The blush that painted her pale cheeks was so bad she could feel the heat from it without even having to look in a mirror to confirm. She couldn't decide if the blush was from embarrassment or her need for him.

"I will show you, but in return, I would like to have you stay tonight so I can feed you breakfast in the morning."

"I have to work at the diner tomorrow morning," she frowned. "I don't even have my uniform with me."

"Can you take the day off?" he asked.

"Oh, no," she shook her head, "I need all the money I make to pay my rent and utilities."

"I'd want you here," he complained. "It's safer that way."

"Safer?" she asked, fear running through her veins. "Are you in danger?"

"We are not accepted by the humans," he growled. "They will do anything to harm us and our families."

"Drake," she said, dropping back into the chair. "Sit down."

"What is it?" he asked, his brow furrowed in worry, but sat down in the chair across from her.

"Humans don't hate your kind," she offered. His eyes narrowed and flashed that golden color again.

"Humans killed my parents," he barked, standing up from his seat as quickly as he had sat down. "You know they want us all dead, right?"

"Not all of us," she said, standing up from her seat. She placed her hand over his heart and smiled. "Not all humans are bad."

"Yes, they are." Drake's mouth parted with a snarl, his fangs were growing in his mouth again, and his hand clamped down on her arm. She was about to jerk away when the pressure became too much, but Drake released her with a curse. "Maybe you should just go home, Tessa."

"Okay," she agreed. "I think that would be a great idea, too."

Jesus Christ, what the fuck was wrong with her? She'd just met him, yet the thought of leaving him sent panic through her veins. Knowing he was pissed off at her made things even worse.

"I'm sorry," he sighed, running his hand over his long, dark hair. "I just don't trust humans. My mind and bear are at odds because you are one of them."

"I assure you," she said, gritting her teeth. "I have no problem with the shifters. I would never hurt one. I've been through enough pain in my life that the thought of hurting another person disgusts me."

"You are a special human," he replied, reaching

up to tuck a strand of hair behind her ear. Every time he touched her, she felt it deep in her soul. "Not all of them are like you."

"*Most* of us are good people," she argued. "I'm sure that in your world you have bad shifter people. It's the same in our world, Drake. Not all shifters are bad, just like not all humans are bad, either."

"Have you seen what happened when the panthers were outed to the humans?" he barked, his mood turning sour. "They captured us and tried to study us!"

"Those were the bad humans, Drake."

"They were human," he continued. "I stick to my own kind, because we are peaceful until we are given a reason not to be."

"Then, maybe you should keep doing that and hiding," she snarled. He was the most frustrating man she'd ever met, and she'd met many over her short twenty-seven years. "I'm leaving."

Drake walked over to his door and held it open wide. "I'm sorry, but you can't convince me to trust humans."

"And that's very sad for you," she sniffled and walked past him, ignoring the growl that rumbled from his chest.

With that, she ran to her car and waited until she closed the door to let the tears flow from her eyes. She'd possibly just met the man of her life…a man she didn't even know she was looking for, and he couldn't look past the fact she was a human.

Chapter 5

Drake shifted as soon as Tessa left his land. His beast trudged through the woods behind his home, looking for peace from the pain in his heart. Tessa was human, and that was a problem. He didn't trust them, and even though his bear had claimed her, he just couldn't get past the fact that her kind had taken his parents from him at the time he had needed his family the most. His bear snarled in agreement.

He couldn't get her scent out of his nose. As a bear, the scent of your mate would always be ingrained in your mind. How could he ever let her go after touching her? His bear brought up images of Drake's human hands on her, and they both remembered the softness of her skin and the velvety touch of her lips against his.

Why had he gotten angry with her and let her go?

He'd just sent his mate home, and he didn't even know where she lived. He didn't know if she would be safe alone. Fear raced up his beast's spine at the thought of her out there without him. What if a human male approached her? Could she protect herself? His bear insisted she couldn't, and he believed his bear over the human side to his brain.

With a roar, he hurried back to his home and shifted as he climbed the stairs of his porch, walking through his home stark naked. When he entered his room, Drake reached for his phone as he pulled on his clothes. Rex answered on the second ring and Drake didn't even wait for a greeting. "We have to find Tessa."

"I thought she was with you?" Rex asked, the sound of music in the background confirming that he was probably at *The Deuce*.

"No, she left ten minutes ago," he snarled. "I told her to leave when she defended her kind. I was angry and shifted when she left. As soon as I made it to the woods, my bear wanted her here. We're worried for her safety against a human male…her ex-husband."

"Why the hell would you send her away?" Rex barked. Drake wondered the same thing.

"I don't know where she lives," Drake cursed, ignoring his brother's question. "I have to find her, Rex. I've made a huge mistake."

"You are a fucking idiot," Gunner yelled through the phone.

"I know I am," he groaned, scooping up the keys to his truck as he rushed out the door. "I'm heading your way."

"Alright, big brother," Rex sighed. "You need

to come to *The Deuce*. This time, don't screw it up."

"Thank you," Drake said as he slid into the seat and cranked the truck.

The drive to the bar took him less than ten minutes. His brothers met him in the parking lot and both of them were smiling from ear to ear, and that just pissed him off. "What the fuck are you smiling about?"

"Found your mate," Gunner shrugged, hooking his thumb over his shoulder. "She's inside having a beer."

"Are you kidding me?" Drake snarled. "You better not be joking, Gunner."

"I would never," he replied, narrowing his eyes. "She's your mate, even if you think she's just a measly human."

"Watch yourself," Drake warned and pushed past his little brother.

He didn't wait for them to follow and marched to the door, pulling it open wide. The first thing he saw as he entered was Tessa sitting at the bar. One of the werepanthers, Dane, was standing by the door, watching over the bar owned by his alpha's mate.

"Drake," Dane nodded. "Nice to see you again."

"Same," Drake said as he passed. It wasn't that he didn't like the cats, but he was more focused on Tessa, his mate.

A snarl caused his upper lip to vibrate when a human male slid onto the barstool next to Tessa. Her long hair floated around her head when she shook it after the male asked her a question. He willed her to send the male away and look up. He wanted her to see him standing there. He wanted her to know that no male would ever touch her again, because the little human was his.

Like she'd heard him, Tessa looked over the male's shoulder and her eyes widened when they connected with his. Drake heard her gasp from across the bar. His eyes narrowed and his beast roared in his mind. The push from his beast was so intense, he felt the skin on his arms bubble with an impending shift. The only thing that kept him from going furry was the fact that he was in public and he valued his secrecy.

The spurs on his boots clanged as he marched toward her. Noises in the bar subsided as Drake approached Tessa and the male suitor with his bear begging to unleash its claws on the male.

"Tessa." His voice held an air of authority, and he was surprised when her body relaxed just the smallest amount. His cock hardened at the idea of her accepting him and the dominance he kept leashed.

"Drake," she said, nervously looking at the male. She glanced at him again, and he knew she saw his eyes were golden. His female turned toward the human male. "You're in his seat."

"Oh, really?" the male said, cocking his head to the side as he turned around on the barstool. One look at Drake and the man hurried to his feet and scrambled away, his bravado deflating with the fear of a predator breathing down his neck. As soon as he was out the door, Drake pushed the stool out of the way and took Tessa's beer into his hands.

"He shouldn't have run," Drake snarled, turning up the beer and finishing off the liquid from the bottle.

"Why?" she asked.

"Bears like to chase their prey," he warned, and set the bottle down hard on the bar. He turned to go after the male, ignoring his brothers as they came to his side.

"Oh, no! Drake!" she gasped as he marched toward the exit.

His bear insisted on finding the male and tearing him to shreds for hitting on Tessa, but as soon as he made it to the parking lot, Rex and Gunner stepped in front of him.

"He's gone," Rex said.

"Drake!" Tessa gasped as she caught up to him. "You better not hurt that man!"

"He's not going to be a problem," Rex chuckled. "Never seen someone run so fast in my life."

"Damn it, Drake," she panted.

"You need to come home with me," he demanded.

"You actually think I'm going to come back to your place after you talked about humans as if they were scum?" Tessa placed her hands on her hips and leaned in to keep yelling at him. "You do realize I'm human, right? Why would I ever go back to your place?"

"Woman," he growled, releasing a heavy sigh.

"I'll be going back to my apartment," she informed him, jerking her arm out of the way when Drake reached for her. He was impressed. She was fast.

"I will be seeing you, my mate," he promised, and watched as she left the lot, turning north to head toward town.

The next morning, Tessa donned her apron and grabbed an order pad from the stack in the diner's kitchen. She was beyond tired after her evening with Drake Morgan. Her mind was still confused and at odds over what she had learned the night before. There were bear shifters, and they didn't want to be outed to the humans.

Fine, she could keep his secret. Not because she was afraid of him, but because he was so adamant about it not being leaked. Drake had a reason for keeping his secret. Tessa understood that more than most. She knew the fear of being found by someone who could harm you.

She'd been running from her ex-husband since the divorce had been finalized three years ago. He'd found her in Tulsa right before Christmas the year before, demanding she return to him. Bradley had beat her nearly to the point of death, and if it hadn't been for someone calling an ambulance, she'd have been dead behind the place where she worked the night shift. Once she recovered, Tessa packed her bags and found her way to Olive Branch, Mississippi. The town was large enough, not everyone would know who she was, but it was small enough, the people she did know kept an eye out for her. Tulley, and her boss at the diner, Gaia, always helped her when they could. They'd been more than nice to her since her arrival.

She'd rented a studio apartment above a shop in the downtown area not long after arriving in Mississippi. Tessa had found it in an ad and fell in love with it immediately. The apartment was secluded, and no one could find her. The entrance was hidden behind a tall shrub at the side of the building, and she had her own parking spot in a gravel driveway in the back.

She worked the afternoon shift at the parts store. Tulley paid her minimum wage, and she was able to keep all of her tips from the diner, plus a small wage. Gaia also gave her free meals when she worked, but that was only four mornings a week.

She could always take an evening job, but since her attack, she didn't care much for leaving a job at night. The money she made covered her rent and utilities, leaving a small amount for food. At night, she usually curled up on the couch in her apartment and watched television until she fell asleep, waking up early to go into work when the sun came up each day. Her only day off was Sunday, and she used that day to go to the local laundromat to wash clothes. She hadn't made any friends in town since she arrived, unless you called Tulley and Gaia her friends.

"How was your evening?" Gaia asked as she entered the dining area.

"It was uneventful," Tessa replied, remembering not to mention the bear shifters. She wouldn't even tell people she knew Drake Morgan if that made him feel safe. For some reason, she felt she needed to protect him and his brothers. As much of an asshole as Drake Morgan could be, she felt something when he touched her. The connection was strong, and Tessa couldn't stop thinking about him.

"What are you doing on your day off, dear?" Gaia continued as they refilled the salt and pepper shakers on each table.

"Probably laundry and sleep, but it all depends on the weather," Tessa told her, knowing on Sunday there was a chance of spring showers. She didn't want to get out in the weather if it was going to turn nasty.

"They're calling for some storms, but later in the day," Gaia offered.

"Great, so no sleeping in," Tessa whined lightheartedly, sliding the full shaker to the middle of the table by the napkins and ketchup bottle.

They worked for another ten minutes before Gaia flipped the sign on the door, telling everyone they were open. A few older men entered the diner, taking their usual seats. Tessa gathered her order pad and smiled as she approached.

"Good morning, gentlemen," she greeted. The men rambled off their order, and Tessa promised to return with coffee.

Gaia seated a couple with a small child as Tessa retuned to drop off the order for the men. The couple was beautiful, and the woman was obviously pregnant with their second child. The man held his daughter close as he looked over the menu. Tessa watched as the woman looked up at her husband and child with so much love on her face, it brought tears to Tessa's eyes.

"That's our local werepanther alpha, Talon Shaw, and his wife, Liberty," Gaia announced as she poured coffee and water for the family.

"They own the bar south of town, right?" she asked, remembering seeing the woman's name on a health inspection report that hung over the bar.

"*The Deuce* is her bar," Gaia nodded.

Tessa waited by the kitchen as their cook, Tony, worked his magic on the grill. She ducked out when a new table was seated, taking their order. When she dropped off food for a lady and her grandson, she took the new table's order and off she went. The couple left after they ate, and for the rest of the day, Tessa couldn't stop thinking about the shifters. It wasn't that she didn't know about them, it was just that she'd been dealing with her own problems when they were found out to be real and not the myths of her childhood.

When she returned home around three that afternoon, Tessa used her phone to look up the shifters on the internet. It wasn't like they had their own websites that told everyone about them. Oh, she found several hate groups who said that the shifters were abominations and spouted religious reasonings, but she just didn't believe any of what they were saying. Not after seeing the werepanther alpha with his mate and meeting Drake Morgan. Yeah, Drake was an asshole at first, but after he'd fed her, something changed. He was…nicer…sort of. Whatever he was, Tessa wanted to learn more about them.

One article on a raid of an island a few months ago caught her attention. Apparently, one of the hate groups had hired scientists to study the shifters they'd kidnapped. They were shut down and several species had been saved. The article did not elaborate on what kind of shifters were found the day it was raided, but other websites indicated black and small brown bears, panthers, and wolves had been found on that island. She wondered if Drake was keeping hidden because of the groups like this one.

She left the diner at noon and hurried home to rest. Saturday nights were always good for a movie on television, and she wasn't disappointed when she found an old classic.

Clouds were darkening as the afternoon faded into evening. The sound of the rain on her apartment window lulled her into a deep sleep. She woke in the middle of the night long enough to turn off the television. She needed to sleep.

The next morning, she woke up at her usual time and started a pot of coffee. The news called for another evening rainstorm, and Tessa hoped she could get all of her chores done before it arrived.

She wondered where Drake was, and if he had been working in his fields. Rex should've had the parts she delivered already installed on the machines they owned.

Why couldn't she stop thinking about him? She'd dreamed of him the past two nights. The dreams were nothing of significance, but he was there, always in the background, keeping a protective eye on her.

Tessa sighed and rinsed out her coffee cup. She wished Drake didn't hate humans as much as he did, and it appeared no matter what she said to try and convince him otherwise would be met with resistance.

"Oh, Drake," she whispered, shaking her head.

Tessa decided to fight the Sunday crowd and do her laundry since she had time. Sitting around analyzing Drake Morgan wasn't going to get things done. Hopefully, he would someday come to his senses and trust humans to a point where he didn't isolate himself on that land.

She gathered her basket and supplies, grabbing her keys as she fumbled with the door handle. Taking the stairs, she slowed as she approached her car. Tears immediately sprung from her eyes at the sight before her. Fear raced up her spine like an untamed wildfire.

On the hood of her car was her cat, Renegade, his blood smeard across the front windshield. Bile rose in the back of her throat as she dropped the basket and ran up the staircase to her apartment. Her hands shook as she tried several times to get her key into the lock. The moment the key slid in and released the mechanism, she ran inside and locked the door. She didn't know who to call. She knew the message was from Bradley, because Renegade was the cat she had to leave behind when she ran away.

Chapter 6

Drake frowned when Tulley's personal cell phone number came up on his caller ID. He wondered why the old man was calling him on a Sunday. What he heard over the line sent a cold chill down his spine.

"Drake," Tulley began, there was an anger in his voice Drake had never heard. "I hate to bother you, but I need your help. Tessa called and she's had quite the fright. I couldn't understand her through all the crying. I'm out of town, and I watch over that girl like she's one of my own. I need someone to check on her. I trust you to do that. Do you mind?"

"Where does she live?" he barked when his beast snarled in his head.

Tulley gave an address to a business in the center of town, telling him to go to the stairwell around the side of the building. Her apartment was above it. Drake hung up and rushed to his truck, yelling for his brother, Gunner, to go with him. Rex was away from their land for the day.

"What the hell is going on?" Gunner asked as he jumped into the truck.

"Something's wrong with Tessa," he snarled and pressed the pedal down to the floor of his truck, hoping he didn't get pulled over by the sheriff as he filled Gunner in on what Tulley had said. His brother cursed several times but sat back and waited for them to arrive at her apartment. Drake was worried what he would find, but the fear of knowing she was hysterical made him even more determined to reach her.

As soon as they arrived, Drake stepped out of his truck and recognized her car. He paused when he looked through the back windshield. Something was splattered on the front one. Gunner cursed as he approached Drake's back. "That's blood."

"Fuck," Drake hollered as he ran toward the car. On the hood was a domestic cat. "Someone slit this cat's throat."

"Who would do that?" Gunner asked.

"Let me get Tessa," he replied, looking up the stairwell behind a tall bush. It led to a top floor apartment, and there was a basket of clothes strewn all over the bottom few steps. Drake stepped over them and took the stairs two at a time. His heavy hand landed on the wooden frame. "Tessa! It's Drake!"

The door opened, and his blonde female fell into his arms. Her tears soaked into his shirt as he scooped her up and moved her over to the couch against the far wall. The apartment was the size of his bedroom. There was a small kitchenette to his left, and another door straight ahead that he assumed was her bathroom.

"Tell me what happened," he ordered, taking her chin with his forefinger.

"It's my ex-husband," she cried. "I had to leave my cat, Renegade, behind when I left him. Now, he's found me, and he's letting me know."

"Jesus," Gunner cursed and turned to walk out the door. "I'll take care of everything outside, Tessa."

"Thank you," she sniffled, then looked up into Drake's eyes. Her hands were still fisted in his shirt as she rested her face back on his chest.

"Tell me about this male," Drake ordered. He wanted to know everything about him so he could find him and kill him for making Tessa cry. Her tears ripped at his soul and this man would pay.

"Bradley Ward," she said, wiping at her eyes. "I divorced him three years ago. He threatened me, and I left town. He found me in Tulsa last Christmas and left me for dead behind the diner I worked at after closing one night."

"You are coming home with us," he decided instantly. "Grab your things."

"I can't do that," she gasped as he stood up and placed her on her feet. "That's asking way too much from you."

"Do as I ask of you, Tessa," he snarled, looking toward the front door. "This isn't an option. If you stay here, he could kill you this time, and I refuse to let that happen."

"Okay, fine," she relented. Drake could see the defeat she felt on her face. Her beautiful blue eyes were red from crying and her face wasn't as bright as it was the night she'd brought the parts to his home and he'd fed her.

His beast snarled in his head. They wanted to take her home and feed her again. It was in their nature to provide and protect, and Drake wanted nothing more than to hide her on his land until he could track down this male and kill him.

Gunner met them at the truck. The cat had been removed and most of the blood had been washed away. Drake turned Tessa's face into his chest as he walked her past the car. "You two go ahead. Rex is on his way to pick me up, and I'll finish cleaning this up while I wait on him. Tessa, your laundry basket is in Drake's truck."

Drake nodded and helped Tessa with the small bag she'd packed into his truck. He buckled her seatbelt and walked around the front of the vehicle, stopping to talk to his brother. "I want this guy found."

"He's yours once we do find him," Gunner promised. "Take your mate home. We will be there in about an hour."

Drake cranked the truck and pulled out of her small driveway. The laundry basket sat between them, and he wanted to toss it into the back of his truck so he could pull her to his side. His need to protect her was the only thing on his mind. The animal that lived inside him wanted the male's blood for the things he'd done to Tessa.

"We are going to talk more about this once I have you in a safe place," Drake stated as he turned for the highway leading toward his property south of town.

"I can talk to you now," she sighed, shaking her head. "I was an idiot and married this guy who promised me everything. It didn't take long before he showed his true colors. He was abusive, plain and simple. It took me some time before I could gather the money to divorce him. When I did, he came after me."

"How many times did he hurt you?" Drake asked, squeezing his hands around the steering wheel.

"Many," she admitted, turning her head to look out the window. She was silent for the longest time, and Drake was about to ask her to go into detail, but she sighed and continued without being prompted. "I'm not going to tell you everything was hearts and flowers. He abused me, and I let him for two years. He's tried to kill me more than just the incident in Tulsa."

"You are very brave for leaving," Drake said through gritted teeth. "But I promise you, if I find him, I will kill that human male."

"Why do I believe you?" she said with a soft chuckle. Drake took his gaze off the road for a second to glance at her face. She was smiling softly as she wiped away the tears. Those tears gutted him. The big, badass bear who could kill a human with just one swipe of his bear paw was affected by the little woman's pain more than he would admit.

"Because you know I'm capable."

"I do."

"You do? How?" he asked, wondering where she had gotten her information. The paranoid side of him wondered if she was associated with the hate groups, but the rational side of him knew she wasn't.

"I looked up information on shifters." Drake saw her shrug out of the corner of his eye, and he was surprised she was so forthcoming with her explanation.

"You did, huh?" he asked, raising a brow and wondering exactly what she'd found.
He didn't know what information was out there on the human's internet. He hoped like hell none of his fellow brother grizzly bears had been found during the raids, and he hoped to keep his secret from the humans for as long as possible. His business and life depended on the secrecy.

"There were wolves, panthers, lions, and black and small brown bears reported in an article," she informed him, turning in her seat. "Are you a black bear?"

"Hah!" he laughed, the mood lightening inside the small space of his truck. "No, little one, I am not."

"Then what are you?" she begged.

"We can talk more after I get you home," he grunted, and glanced at her out of the corner of his eye. She was his mate and trust was something he was going to have to give over to her at some point. But when? When would be the time to tell her?

Now, Drake. You need to trust her.

"Oh, okay," she said in defeat, but his mate was inquisitive and kept up with the questions. "Will you show me this time?"

"I will," he promised on a nod. "After I feed you and bathe you."

"Bathe me?" She narrowed her eyes when he flashed her a soft smile. "I can do that on my own."

"If you insist," he drawled as he passed the werepanther-owned bar. "I'll show you where everything is in our home."

The drive to his place was silent, and he wanted to reach over and touch her again. His bear insisted on it, but he refrained.

Drake urged Tessa to eat the meal he prepared for her. She sat at his kitchen table and ate all she could before pushing the plate away. He looked up from his own food, inspecting her plate and nodding when he was satisfied she'd consumed enough.

"I want to know more about your ex-husband," he demanded.

"I trust too easily," she sighed. God, how stupid was she? Bradley had given her everything her heart desired, but he was a monster beneath the proper gentleman he showed to everyone else.

"What happened with your former mate, Tessa?" he pressed.

"Oh whew," she sighed, unsure of how she was going to tell him about her time with Bradley. "I don't even know where to start."

"From the beginning will work," Drake grunted. "I need to know what I'm facing from this male."

"I met Bradley when I was working at a club in Chicago," she began, squeezing her hands tight where she had them hidden beneath the table. No matter how much she tightened the muscles in her body, Tessa's right leg began to bounce as the memories flashed through her mind. "He was there with his friends from work. I knew he had to be some sort of corporate executive by the way he dressed. He was polite, but he was also very forward. His chivalry and dominant nature appealed to me."

Tessa paused to look up into Drake's eyes. She wasn't sure how much she should tell him. The lifestyle she craved wasn't always accepted by other people. Plus, he was a shifter. Would he understand her explanations?

"Go on," he urged, leaning back in his chair. Tessa looked away when the muscles in his arms flexed. Drake's strength radiated with his every move, and she ached from imagining the things he could do with those arms; like holding her tight…protecting her.

"Over the next few weeks, he came into the club every other night," she said. "He finally asked me out, and I accepted."

God, she'd had some rose-colored glasses on with that one. Bradley had promised her the world, even gave her a glimpse of it for a time.

"He pampered me and took care of me in the way that I craved." She paused, weighing her words. "We married a year later, and that's when he turned into a monster."

"A monster?" Drake growled. "What type of monster?"

"I…I don't even know how to explain this to you," she stammered, looking into his eyes. They weren't flashing gold like they did when he'd bared his fangs at her or his brothers, and she assumed that meant he was calm. Tessa still wasn't entirely sure how shifters worked, or what their species was like.

"Tell me," he urged.

"He fulfilled all of my fantasies, but he was a sadist." She paused when Drake's eyes narrowed. "He hurt me…a lot."

"He didn't accept your safewords?" he asked. Tessa gasped softly when she realized he knew exactly what she was talking about. "You are a submissive?"

"*Only* in the bedroom," she blushed, but straightened her spine. "Bradley thought he could control me and my actions. I wasn't allowed out of his sight, and after I begged to go see my mom, he punished me when I wasn't home by the agreed upon time."

"Punished you how?" Drake asked, leaning forward. The shifter laid his hand on top of hers, and Tessa swore she felt strength from the connection. He'd told her he couldn't control her mind, but this feeling she had when they touched made her think he had some sort of magic inside him.

"Are you calming me?"

"It's the touch of a mate," he smiled sadly. "I will explain that to you *after* you finish telling me everything about this male, Bradley."

"It started about nine months after we married."

She had to stop for a second, feeling tears well up in her eyes. It was hard to relive the past, but she needed to tell him. No one should live in shame for being a victim of domestic violence. "He would chain me to the bedroom wall and use a belt on me until he wasn't angry anymore. No matter how many times I used my safeword, he wouldn't stop."

"I will kill him," Drake vowed, his eyes flashing that golden hue. Tessa flipped her hand over and clasped his when his fangs grew to sharp points.

"He was eventually fired from his job, and he turned violent with anyone who looked at him wrong. I found illegal drugs in his bedside drawer."

"What did you do?"

"It took me just over two years after that to escape him," she said, squeezing his hand. "I'm okay now."

"No, Tessa," he growled, his upper lip quivering from the rumble that bubbled out of his chest. "No, you are not okay. He knows where you are, and that son of a bitch means business."

"I know," she worried. "He threatened me the night he found me in Tulsa."

"What did he say?" Drake pushed. Tessa felt at ease with him. There was something about Drake that made her body relax and the anxiety in her mind float away into nothingness.

"He kept telling me that he wouldn't kill me

yet. He wanted me to suffer while he repeatedly punched me in the face and kicked me in the ribs." She stopped and used her free hand to touch the spot on her right side where Bradley had broken three of her ribs.

"What have the human authorities done?"

"Nothing," she admitted. "I told the hospital I'd fallen down some stairs."

"Jesus, Tessa," Drake snarled.

"I've been on the run ever since."

"There will be no more running," he stated, releasing her hand and slashing it through the air for emphasis. "You are staying here with me."

"I can't…" She paused when he stood to his full height. Drake took her chin with his large hand and tilted her face so he could look her in the eye.

"Tessa, do as you're told," he ordered with power behind his voice. It was a power she craved, and that alone made Tessa submit.

"Yes, Sir."

"I promise you, from this day forth, I will protect you in all ways. In my world, we are destined to be with one mate, and it's for life. My bear has chosen you, and I know you don't understand yet, but you will."

"Why do I keep having these feelings when you touch me?" she asked, blinking a few times to keep the tears at bay.

"What are you feeling?" he asked, coming around to take her by the hand. Tessa stood up and pressed the palms of her hands to his chest. There was that feeling again. An invisible strength wrapped around her.

"I feel safe," she explained, finally looking up into his eyes.

"It's our connection."

"This mate thing you keep speaking of?" she pressed.

"Yes, little one." He smiled and tilted her head to capture her lips. It didn't matter that she didn't know this man. He'd shown up at her place after Tulley had called him to come check on her. Drake, being the ultimate asshole during their first meeting, treated her with kindness and respect.

"Are you going to trust me with your secret now?" she asked.

"I will show you. Come with me."

She pushed the chair back to its rightful place under the table. Drake called out for his brothers who had retired to their rooms and took her hand. Tessa felt the stirrings of lust again when he touched her. She didn't know why that was happening, even though Drake promised her he wasn't making her feel that way.

"Tessa," Rex, the one with the long, dark-blond hair, smiled. "Drake?"

"I'm going to shift," he announced, much to his brother's shock. Rex's eyes popped wide and he looked between the two.

"Are you sure?" Rex asked, narrowing his eyes. Tessa had a feeling Rex was confused by Drake's eagerness to shift in front of a human. She wanted nothing more than to put them all at ease. The last thing she would ever do was tell their secret.

"Yes," he growled, his eyes glowing bright. Tessa started to say something, but paused when the other brother, Gunner, entered the room.

"Come on, Tessa," Gunner laughed. "You can stand with me, and I'll protect you from him."

"Protect me?" she gasped, attempting to pull her hand from Drake's tight hold.

"I won't hurt you," Drake growled and turned toward his brother. "Don't scare her."

"Drake," she whispered, trying her best to slow her heart rate. "What's going to happen?"

"I'm going to take you outside and leave you with my brothers while I shift," he explained. "If you'd like, you can touch me. My beast will know it's you the entire time."

"You will?" she asked, frowning. "Can you hear me when you…shift?"

"Yes," he replied, opening the back door. For the middle of March, the evenings were still brisk. Tessa shivered from the cool air, and Drake stepped back inside the door to grab a denim jacket to drape over her shoulders. "I can hear and understand you, but I won't be able to speak with you."

"O…okay," she stammered.

Drake released her, and both of his brothers came to stand beside her; Rex to her left and Gunner to her right. Drake removed his shirt and Tessa swallowed a lump in her throat. He was broad shouldered and tattooed across his chest and down his left arm. "You may want to look away for this part."

"Are you getting nak…" she gasped and closed her eyes.

"Our clothes don't shift with us," Gunner snickered. "You can look now."

Tessa turned around as Drake's body shimmered. He twisted his head from side to side and hair sprouted from his human skin. She watched as his body grew in size and his face began to reshape into something else. His nose grew and those fangs she'd already seen became longer. His hands swelled and long claws erupted from the tips. Within seconds, a huge grizzly bear stood where Drake's human form had been.

"Oh, my," she breathed out, clutching her chest.

Drake, the large grizzly bear, huffed and took a step toward the porch. Tessa automatically took a step back. Gunner turned toward her with a frown. "Go say hello, Tessa."

"He knows it's me, right?" she asked, needing reassurance.

"Drake and his bear know it's you," Gunner promised. "We know our mates through sight, touch, and scent. He would be able to find you like a needle in a haystack if it was ever needed. Now, go on." Gunner held his hand out as if he were offering her up for a meal.

Drake's bear sat on his backside and waited patiently. She took one step forward and then another. As she approached, the bear laid down on its belly, resting his massive head on his front paws. The top of his head was a paler brown than the rest of his body. Tessa still couldn't believe she was face to face with such a deadly predator. If this had been in the wild, she'd have been bear food already.

"Drake?" she whispered as she approached. The bear lifted its head and sniffed the air. A soft rumble came from its chest as she slowly put her hand in front of him. "I don't know what to do."

The bear nuzzled her palm and closed its eyes. He rutted into her hand, silently telling Tessa to touch his fur. With shaking fingers, she ran her hand over the top of his head. The fur felt bristly and rough, and the tips were a bit white like the real grizzlies in the wild. She moved from his head to his ears and ran her fingers over them, noticing the fur there was a bit softer. She couldn't believe she was touching this massive animal. The grizzly had to be at least eight hundred pounds.

"I can't believe I'm touching a grizzly bear, and he's not trying to eat me." Tessa knelt in front of him, thinking she was crazy. If she hadn't seen Drake shift, she would've thought it was a trick. In fact, her mind was still trying to catch up with what she'd seen. "Is it really you, Drake?"

The bear growled and nodded his head. Drake's bear pressed his nose into her belly and rubbed his head back and forth. Tessa was frozen and didn't know what else to do. When she looked over her shoulder for Rex and Gunner, they were gone.

Tessa let out a short gasp when the bear nudged her enough to knock her onto her side, but she needn't have worried. Drake's massive bear arm broke her fall. She let out a short laugh when he rested his head over her stomach but didn't put any of his weight on her.

"Are you going to keep me here all night?" she giggled when he snorted.

The bear nuzzled into her belly and closed his eyes. She finally relaxed as he did and just looked up at the stars. How the hell had she ended up falling for a shifter? Why in the world did she feel so safe here on their farm?

"Your touch soothes me," she whispered and ran her fingers over the course fur on top of his head.

Drake's bear huffed and made a satisfied noise in his throat. She didn't know what made her want to tell him everything about her life, but she did, and as she touched him, the words tumbled out of her mouth.

"I've been living on the edge of fear for the past year. Being here on your land brings me peace. I don't even know how to explain it."

Drake's bear shimmered and within seconds, a naked man laid next to her. She didn't dare avert her eyes from him to give him privacy, but she did move her hand from his head to the side of his face, running her fingers through his short beard.

"Our species isn't like yours," he began. "We are compassionate, but also very dangerous when it comes to protecting our family. In my world, you find your mate, and love comes over time. When a werebear finds his female, she is pampered and treated with respect. The females of a clan are like royalty, and they are our top priority."

"Are there female bears?" she asked, genuinely curious.

"Yes," he nodded, pausing for a moment to rest his head on his palm when she rolled to the side. Tessa missed his head on her belly but didn't voice it. "We haven't heard of any female bears in our area."

"Why me?" she continued with the questions. "Why didn't you go looking for your mate in your own species?"

"That's not the way it works." He shook his head. "Our destined mate is just that…destined. We believe Mother Nature will provide us with our soul mates when she is ready. Rex and Gunner have tried going to other dens to meet females, but it's the skin to skin contact that tells us we've found her."

"So, you just go around touching women?"

"No," Drake chuckled. Tessa's body heated from seeing the allusive smile on his face. Drake was grumpy, and he was demanding. When he let his guard, and his hate for humans, down, there was a softness about him. "We socialize with them, and if we feel a connection, we would ask the female to touch. If our bears decline them, we move on."

"I wish humans had that," she mumbled as she stared off into the sky. If she'd been a bear, maybe she wouldn't have fallen for Bradley's charms and married him. It would've saved her all those years of her life she'd never get back.

"Humans are ungrateful for their partners," Drake huffed.

"There's a lot of divorce in my world, because people jump into marriage too quickly," she agreed.

"Females give us young," Drake continued, using the back of his knuckle to trace over her arm. She shivered from the contact, but he didn't notice. "They continue our line while loving us unconditionally."

"Can you have children with humans?" she asked, immediately blushing. "I'm sorry. I'm being too forward."

"No, it's okay," he replied. "We cannot cross-breed with humans."

"Oh," she frowned. Where had this wanting children question come from anyway? Tessa sure as hell wasn't ready to find a man and start a family. She could barely make ends meet as it was with her two jobs. "I was just curious."

"I noticed that about you," he said, pulling her hand. "Let's go back inside and I'll draw you a bath. You've had a long day."

"A bath sounds lovely," she sighed, and stood up, blushing when she looked down at his naked body. She didn't mean to look, but it just happened and well, he was erect, and huge…and Tessa turned her head quickly. Drake chuckled and started walking.

"Nudity is normal for shifter kind," he offered.

"Well, I'm not used to that," she replied.

"You'll get used to it," he said as they reached the porch. Drake opened the door for her and they entered to find the house empty. Rex and Gunner were gone. "Get your bag and come to my room."

Tessa picked up the bag she'd packed from where Drake had placed it by the front door. When she turned around, he was pulling on a pair of jeans, but left his chest bare. As her eyes roamed his body, she felt stirrings of lust for him. Was that the connection he talked about between mates?

She tucked her chin and followed him down one of three hallways. As they traveled, the floor sloped as if the house was going into the ground. "Is this underground?"

"We hibernate most of the winter," he supplied. "When my brothers and I built the house, we designed it to have our own living areas and bedrooms below ground so we could have our own place with our mates but stay close to each other for safety."

"Wait," she froze. "You hibernate during the winter? Like the wild grizzlies?"

"Well, we sleep a lot," he smirked. "If we have a mate, and she is carrying our cub, we pamper her during that time."

"From what I remember from school, grizzlies have their babies during the late winter, right?" She was Ms. Twenty-Questions with him, but he was answering, and that was better than his asshole attitude the first time they'd interacted.

"Our females will give birth during the hibernation period, and we deliver them here at home," he answered. "All males are trained to deliver their young when they come of age."

"*You* deliver your own children?" she gasped.

"We've delivered our own cubs since the beginning of time. The knowledge is passed down from father to son."

"Okay," she said, letting the information sink in. They were very self-sufficient, and she liked that about them. Although, the thought of having a child at home with no medicine did kind of freak her out.

Inside the first room was a large living area, complete with a large, dark-brown sofa and love seat. A huge flat-screen television was mounted to the wall by the door. "This is my living space."

"It's cozy," she added, trying to lighten his mood. As she looked to the left, in the corner was a small kitchenette with only a sink, short countertop with a two-burner stove, and a refrigerator in the area. Tessa assumed they cooked all of their meals in the main kitchen and used this for their winter hibernation.

"My room," he mumbled as he walked over to another closed door. Inside was a large, metal framed bed. There were slats for the headboard, and a thick comforter the same color as his couch was pulled back as if he'd made his bed that morning and drew back one side of the covers so he could climb in as soon as he was ready for the night. A large chest of drawers and two side tables were the only other furniture in the room. "Let me have your bag and you can make yourself comfortable. I'll sleep on the couch tonight."

"Thank you," she said. Tessa climbed on the bed and began removing her shoes. She sighed when the material formed to her body. The old couch she slept on in her apartment was not comfortable at all. This bed was like laying on a cloud, and she yawned just imagining the wonderful night's sleep she would soon be getting on it.

"I'll draw your bath now," he said, disappearing into the bathroom. Shortly after, the water started and she lay back on the pillow, inhaling when she caught his woodsy scent.

Tessa closed her eyes for a moment, trying to dislodge the images of her cat murdered and the remains left on her car windshield. Why was Bradley doing this? Why wouldn't he leave her alone? A lone tear trailed down her cheek, and she jerked when a warm finger wiped it away.

"Everything will be okay, Tessa," Drake said as she opened her eyes to see him standing over her. "I will never let him hurt you again."

"You can't be with me all the time, Drake," she replied, shaking her head when his eyes glowed. "I have to work."

"Eventually, you will be living here," he stated, his eyes cooling to their usual brown hue. "When that time comes, you will have no need to work, and if you do, you can work for me from home."

"I still have my own bills to pay," she argued. "What you're offering me is a fairy tale, Drake. I have to be realistic here."

"Then I will come and sit at that human diner and the parts shop while you work to offer protection," he confirmed. "You will not be alone one second of the day."

"There is no way you can stand being around humans for that long," she replied, rolling her eyes.

"I've done a protection detail for the panthers before. This will be less painful, I promise you," he teased with a smirk.

"If you're sure," she said, closing her eyes. "I trust you to keep me safe, Drake. By no means am I a wimp, but I know for a fact, I cannot protect myself from Bradley. He's so much bigger than I am."

"Bigger than me?" Drake asked.

"No, not bigger than you," she said, patting his chest. "You are the biggest man I know."

"Male," he corrected with a grunt. "We call ourselves males."

"Sorry," she giggled. "You are the biggest *male* I know."

"Damn right." He nodded and took her hand. "Time to bathe."

"Yes, Sir." She smiled and let him lead her to the bathroom where he released her hand and closed the door. She eyed the lock and decided against twisting the dial, trusting Drake to let her bathe in peace.

The tub was huge and deep, and the bathroom was spacious enough for a big man…male like Drake. The custom cabinets were a dark brown like the ones in the main house, and the countertops were beige. It made the room feel inviting with the matching paint on the wall.

She slipped off her clothes and tested the water with her big toe. The temperature was perfect, and when she climbed in, the water came up to her chin. Oh, God. She could get used to this.

It broke her heart that Drake hated humans so much. He didn't elaborate as to why, but maybe he'd eventually open up and tell her everything. She wanted to know more about him, his brothers, and this secret life he led.

Did Tulley know about him being a shifter? Was that why her boss had called Drake when she called him for help?

She guessed it didn't matter at this point, because she was already in over her head with the feelings he was causing inside her heart.

Chapter 7

Tessa ignored the stares from the patrons of the diner as she entered with Drake and Rex behind her. She really didn't want them to follow her to work, but she wasn't going to argue with Drake because Bradley was in the area. Her hands began to shake and she worried them by twisting her palms against each other when she entered the backroom to grab her apron. A gasp burst from her chest when she turned around and Drake was right behind her. He immediately took her shaking hands into his and frowned. "Don't be scared."

"It's kind of hard not to be." Tessa bowed her head and sighed. "I still vividly remember the last time I saw him."

"I'm sorry this happened to you," he sympathized. "Come here."

Tessa gladly fell into his hold. The touch sent that odd sensation through her body. The idea of a species knowing who they were destined to be with for eternity made Tessa question everything she'd ever known about being a human. "I wish I was a bear so I could protect myself when he comes for me."

Drake's body froze, but his hold did not waver. Tessa didn't know if she'd said anything wrong. Maybe telling him she wanted to be a bear was frowned upon in his shifter world? She still didn't know everything about them, and she sure as hell wasn't going to ask any more questions. She'd already been too inquisitive with him when she'd found out.

Oh, but she wanted to ask questions.

"Your former mate will never touch you," he vowed, kissing the top of her head. "I'm going to grab a table in a corner so I'm out of your way. Will you bring me some coffee?" The question was posed with a sexy smirk, and she wanted so bad to rub her thumb over his bottom lip. Instead, she gave him a wink and left the backroom with him following.

Rex was waiting down the hallway and stepped aside as she passed. Tessa found it odd and had noticed that little quirk recently with his brothers. They *never* touched her, or even got close to her in any way.

Drake and Rex took their seats and Tessa got to work. The diner was already open, and Gaia was taking an order out to a table. When she returned, the older woman had a smile on her face. Her wrinkles pulled at the corners as her eyes brightened. "I see you have a male suitor."

"He's just a friend," she shrugged.

"Don't lie to me, Tessa," Gaia scolded. "Tulley called me."

"Great," Tessa sighed.

"If the Morgan men want to watch over you for a while," she began, inclining her head toward Drake, "then you let them."

"You know them?" Tessa asked, wide-eyed. She thought they hated humans.

"I knew their mother," Gaia said in a rush, ducking her head. She wouldn't look Tessa in the eye. "I have a table to serve. Get Drake and Rex some coffee, please."

"Yes, ma'am," she replied. *That was weird.* Tessa wondered how Gaia knew Drake's mother, and if she knew that they were shifters.

Tessa filled two coffee cups and grabbed the sweetener and cream to take to the table where the two men were sitting. Drake watched her as she crossed the diner. His eyes heated, and there was a very faint, golden glow to them. She wondered what his bear was thinking, and if it was okay with being in this environment.

"Excuse me," Rex said with a smile as she set the cups down. She stepped out of the way as he pushed the chair far away and stood up.

Rex looked like Drake, but his hair was lighter. The patrons in the diner were not oblivious to their presence. Both men were huge in comparison to the average human. Drake was well over six feet tall, and Rex matched him in height. Gunner was only slightly shorter, but by no means was he smaller.

"Why do Rex and Gunner stay so far away from me?" she asked as she set the creamer in the middle of the table.

Drake grunted and looked around the diner to see if there was anyone within hearing distance before he answered, "Because once we mate, if a male touches you, it will hurt you."

"Hurt me?" she pressed.

"A male's touch will be painful." He shook his head sadly. "It's said to feel like you've been burned."

"Oh, no," she shook her head, "I don't want that, Drake."

"In my world, males don't touch mated females," he promised. "It's bred into us that we only touch a female who is mated if she is in trouble."

"Then how long does it last? This burning sensation?" Tessa continued. She'd told herself not to keep asking questions, but she'd make an exception to this rule. This sounded important.

"Until her mate touches her to ease the pain," he replied, taking a sip of coffee. "Can we not talk about this here? The diner is filling up."

"Are you okay with being here?" she asked, lowering her voice. "Is *he* okay being around this many people?" She indicted her meaning by pointing to Drake's chest. The last thing she wanted to do was mention anything about him being a shifter in public.

"I'm going to be just fine, little one," he drawled.

"I'll have more questions later," she warned with a smile and turned to leave, but not before she saw a sexy smirk on his lips.

Gunner pulled up the information on Tessa he'd found online. She'd been married to Bradley Ward for around three years before filing for divorce. There was no record of any arrests on either one of their parts during that time.

However, Bradley Ward had a laundry list of arrests after Tessa left him. His crimes were drug and violence related. He'd been charged with possession a few times, assault twice, and he was still out roaming the streets.

If that had been a bear shifter and he'd laid his hands on his mate, or any female for that matter, the clan would've killed him on the spot. They didn't treat women with anything other than the utmost respect. Hell, if Gunner had a mate, she'd be treated like a goddamn queen!

Tessa was a beautiful woman, and exactly what his big, grumpy brother needed. Gunner wouldn't say it out loud, because Drake would surely kick his ass, but since Tessa had showed up on their land, Drake had been calmer, less…well, grumpy. Whatever needed to be done to get those two to accept each other, he was all for making it happen.

This ex-husband of hers was going to be a problem, and if Drake kept his eye on Tessa, Rex and Gunner could find him and take him out without the female knowing. The last thing they wanted to do was upset the female in any way.

Gunner closed his laptop and grabbed his hat. It was time to get out into the field to plant, and he was already burning daylight. He'd have to work for the next few weeks to get the seeds in the ground while Drake watched over his mate.

"We need to be getting back to the land," Drake

mumbled as Tessa walked away from the table they'd been at all morning.

"Gunner is already planting," Rex confirmed. "He's been out since five."

It was just coming up on noon, and Tessa was finishing her shift. Gaia, her boss and owner of the diner, came by and cleaned away what was left of their lunch. She gave Drake and Rex a nod, and the sparkle in her eye wasn't missed when she turned away.

"She's always watched out for us," Rex smiled.

"That she has," Drake replied, watching his mother's best friend move around as if she was still a young female. If he remembered right, Gaia was close to fifty, and had owned the diner since he was in his teens. She had to have been barely twenty when she acquired the place. Not once had she ever missed a day opening the diner in all the years she'd owned it.

"I'm ready," Tessa announced as she approached the table. Drake stood and took her hand. Tessa waved at Gaia over her shoulder and returned to her position close to Drake's side.

Outside, the sun was shining bright, but there was a slight chill to the air. Tessa shivered as she nervously looked around the parking lot. Rex took his keys and walked ahead to unlock the truck. Drake's eyes cautiously scanned the area. His bear wasn't on edge, and he trusted his beast to warn him if something was amiss. The only fear he felt was from Tessa.

A shifter's senses were heightened above what humans experienced, or at least that was what he'd been told. The humans couldn't smell lies and danger like his kind. In the heat of a fight with an enemy, bears could taste the fear of their opponent on their tongues. It was a taste of victory.

"In ya go, little one," Drake said, lifting Tessa into his tall truck. She buckled her seatbelt as he closed the door, remaining quiet while Rex shook Drake's hand and left them alone to drive his own truck back to the farm.

"Can I see him again? The bear?" she asked with a soft blush on her face.

"You like him?" Drake beamed, laughing when his bear made a satisfied sound in his mind.

"I do," she grinned. "I mean, if that's okay?"

"Yes, Tessa," he agreed, "it's okay. We can go play in the woods behind the house after dinner."

"I'd like that," she offered, and turned to look out the window of his truck. "I enjoy the forest. It soothes me."

If seeing his bear brought her peace, he would shift every day. Tessa didn't understand his world, but he knew she was going to be his end game. The human was his mate, regardless of how much he hated them and what they'd done to his family.

Maybe she was right. Maybe not all humans were bad. Tessa was kind and gentle. After watching her work today, he realized that the humans who ate at the diner were decent. Not once were there any altercations. Not that Gaia would allow any of that to happen in her business, but regardless, everyone greeted each other with a warm smile and a handshake.

Drake looked in the mirror as they pulled out of the lot. Gaia was standing by the door and nodded in his direction. She smiled and turned to walk away. He knew things about her that no one else did, and he and his brothers were tasked to keep that secret safe.

"How did your mother know Gaia?" Tessa asked, biting her lip. Drake stared at her for a moment before turning to look at the road.

"My mother worked for her at the diner for a few years," Drake explained. He wasn't lying. His mother had worked for Gaia when he was a teenager.

"What was her name?" Tessa continued.

"Maria." He swallowed hard. Just hearing her name fall from his lips caused a sadness to squeeze his heart. "My father's name was Amell."

"Thank you for telling me." She smiled and continued to stare out the window.

"Tulley has given you the week off with pay," Drake announced. He knew it was best not to tell her while she was at the diner. One thing he'd noticed about Tessa was that she was a proud female and wanted to earn everything she had.

"What?" she barked. "Oh, no, no, no. I can't accept that."

"Too late," Drake shrugged. "He's already put it in your account."

"Damn it," she swore. "Tulley has been so good to me. I don't know if I'll ever be able to repay him for the things he's done for me."

"I've known Tulley for a long time," Drake said as he turned south on the two-lane highway south of town. The drive would take a good twenty minutes, and his mate's scent of honeysuckle was already driving him insane with lust. Her soft sighs and thick legs in her denim jeans wasn't helping much either. "He's a good man."

"For a human?" she asked, looking over at him with a smirk.

"For a human," he agreed.

"See, you aren't as grumpy as you played it off when we first met," she teased, waving her hand to indicate his large body.

"Oh, no, little one," he grinned. "I assure you, I can be very, very grumpy."

"When?" she pressed. The little human was playing with fire. She didn't know not to test the beast, but she was, and he wanted to play.

"When I'm hungry," he began, ticking off all

the things that irritated him. "When humans come on my land. Ahhh, and when my female teases me."

"I'm your female?" she asked with a grin.

"Yes, Tessa Ward," he answered. "You are."

Tessa nodded and continued to stare out the window. Drake would occasionally glance over at her, and he swore he could see her mind churning. He chuckled to himself as he wondered what questions she'd have for him at dinner. He was surprised when he realized he was looking forward to whatever she had to say.

When they arrived at his home, Gunner was just coming from the barn. He'd been in the field all day, and Drake was anxious to find out what he'd learned about Tessa's ex. When his baby brother made eye contact, Drake frowned. Gunner shook his head slightly, telling him now was not a good time to talk about the male.

Whatever Gunner had found wasn't good.

Tessa walked ahead of Drake and entered the house. She made an excuse to shower, and he waited until she descended into his room to head back outside to meet his brother. Rex had arrived already, and the two of them were waiting on the porch.

"What did you find out?"

"All I could find was public records," Gunner cursed. "This guy has been in a lot of trouble the last three years. He's been arrested for minor drug charges and two fights. I don't know why the humans haven't kept him in jail."

"Because he hasn't hurt someone bad enough for them to keep him," Rex answered, his voice lowering to a deathly growl.

"I can't find anything about his current whereabouts," Gunner continued. "Our best hope would be to talk to the sheriff."

"Hmmm," Drake growled. He had weird trust issues with their sheriff. He didn't care that the male was a Watcher, a guardian angel sent to protect the panthers. Drake didn't care much for the male, but he needed him. It was more important to keep Tessa safe than his aversion to anyone coming on his land. "I guess I should call Sheriff Lynch."

"I would advise it," Gunner said, raising his hand when Drake started to speak. "He's our only hope of getting more information on the male."

"I'll see if I can get a face to face meeting with him," Drake promised. "Right now, my mate needs food and she wants to go for a walk in the woods before dark."

"We will leave you two alone," Rex offered.

"No," Tessa said from the door. All three men turned as she was coming out the door. "Please have dinner with us."

"Yes, have a meal with us," Drake agreed.

"Please?" Tessa repeated. "I haven't had much

time to get to know you. I'd like to spend some time with everyone."

"We can do that." Rex nodded and pushed his brother playfully. "Go cook, little man."

"Man, fuck you," Gunner began, but stopped abruptly when Drake narrowed his eyes. "Sorry."

"No need to be sorry," she laughed. "I say 'fuck' a lot when I'm mad."

All three of them stared at her with wide eyes. Drake couldn't believe she had cursed like it was nothing. Maybe this human female really was meant to be in his and his brothers' lives? She sure was making him start to rethink his disgust of humans.

Chapter 8

Drake refused to let Tessa lift a finger when it came to dinner. She wanted nothing more than to help them since she was a guest in their home, but the brothers refused her help and Drake banished her to the small living room in the main part of the house.

She clicked on the television and found the local news station just as the weather was coming on. Rain was coming later in the week, and the temperatures were going to hover right around the sixty-degree mark. Spring was coming, and she was ready for the warmth of summer.

"Would you like some wine?" Drake asked from the kitchen.

"Actually, yes," she called out. "I would love some."

When was the last time she'd had a drink? It seemed like forever since she'd had a night where she could just relax. Since Tulley had given her the week off, Tessa was now off for the day after her shift at the diner ended at noon. Otherwise, she'd have not been home until six or seven, preferring to eat whatever she could find and go directly to bed.

Drake returned with a glass of white wine for

her and a bottle of beer for himself. He sat next to her and rested his ankle on his knee. He was still wearing his dark-brown boots with the spurs attached. She'd noticed he wore them a lot, and she liked to hear them clang with each step he took. The rhythmic sound was soothing.

"So, bear man," Tessa joked, "I kinda like the spurs." She leaned over, and using just her index finger, spun the tarnished metal at the back of his heel.

"Well," Drake flirted, "you never know when you're going to need to mount something."

The laugh that bubbled up from her chest caused Drake to chuckle beside her. He was a slow-talking southern man with expressive eyes and a sexy smile. That was…whenever she could get him to smile.

"What's for dinner?" she asked, sniffing the air. She couldn't quite make out what it was, but it didn't matter. It smelled delicious.

"Chicken Marsala," he answered. "Gunner is a pretty damn good cook, and we've learned to trust him not to kill us. So, he's in charge of dinner."

"I'd like to cook for y'all one night," she offered. "If you don't mind."

"That would be welcomed," he began, "but you are on your feet all day. Gunner will cook." He said it like his words were final, and from what she'd learned about Drake Morgan, he liked things left alone. Change wasn't a part of his life.

"I can cook," she argued. "Gunner is working the fields while you watch me all day."

"It's in our nature to care for our females," he reminded her.

"Do your females do *anything*?" she asked. From the way Drake talked, the females of his den would be lazy and unproductive. Tessa didn't want to do nothing all day.

"They work," he assured her. "My mother worked at the diner, and eventually started working in the office once my father begged her. Our business was booming and he needed help. If a mate wants to work, she can, but we males prefer she rest when she's not."

"Well, that's just crazy," Tessa chuckled. "I will cook tomorrow night. Do you like pork?"

"We're bears, Tessa," he pointed out, his eyes heating as he looked her over. "We'll eat everything."

Tessa took her glass of wine and turned it up for a healthy gulp. She liked when he teased and flirted with her. The big, grumpy bear was growing on her.

"Food's ready!" Gunner hollered from the kitchen.

Drake held out his hand to help her up from the couch. He didn't release his hold as they walked.

There was a warmth to his calloused hands that seeped into her body. His touch made her feel safe.

"Thank you," she said as Drake pulled out her chair. She took her seat and Drake slid into the one beside her. Rex and Gunner sat across from them. The two heads of the table were empty.

"Go ahead," Drake encouraged, relaxing in his seat.

Tessa remembered their pride at letting the women in their home eat first. She plated her food and cut into the first bite. When she looked up, the men were staring at her. Making a sound of approval, she nodded and quickly swallowed her food. "This is delicious. Please, eat."

Gunner smiled widely and waved for his brothers to go first. Satisfied with her response, Drake dug into his food. Rex kept his head down as he did the same.

"Tell us about your life before you met this human male," Gunner blurted, causing Drake to glare over his beer bottle. Tessa took a sip of wine and set her glass down with shaky hands.

"I'm from Chicago, but moved to the panhandle of Florida after my divorce," she began, taking a moment to keep from getting emotional over missing her family. Bonnie Holland, her mother, and Ross, her older brother, were the only family she had contact with anymore. "My mother and brother are there. They moved with me when the divorce from Bradley was final. He threatened to hurt them, as well. So, I moved to Tulsa to keep them safe."

"Have you talked to your family at all?" Rex asked, finally looking up from his plate. She hadn't spent much time with him, but she liked him. His eyes flashed gold, and she placed her hands in her lap to squeeze them together. She wouldn't show fear around them. She'd done too much of that with Bradley.

"I called my mother after Bradley attacked me in Tulsa," she admitted. God, her mother had been so upset, she flew straight from Pensacola to come help her. "She came to Oklahoma, and as soon as I was healed enough, I sent her home. I told my mom I was going to run again, and when things were okay, I would call her."

"Have you talked to her since you've been here?" Drake pressed, reaching over to take her hand under the table. He didn't mention anything about the way she wrung them with her nervousness.

"I have." She smiled sadly. "I only talk to her every few months, because I don't want anyone knowing where I am."

"What about your father?" Gunner asked as he paused in consuming his meal fit for a king.

"We don't speak," she said, gritting her teeth.

"Why not?" Drake asked, moving his body

closer to her. He held a protective posture as he waited for her reply.

"Because he is the one who told Bradley where I was in Tulsa," she growled.

The three men around her exploded out of their chairs. Drake, Rex, and Gunner started yelling about fathers taking care of their daughters. All three men bared their fangs as they cursed. The skin around their eyes bubbled as if they were on the verge of shifting like Drake had done the night before.

"Please," she begged, hoping she could stop them from turning into bears in their own home. "Sit down."

"Your own father sent that human to hurt you!" Drake was so angry. Tessa shivered from the power he gave off with his hatred of what she'd told him.

"There's more to the story," Tessa promised, reaching out to touch Drake's hand. He relaxed and looked down at her. "Please, sit."

Tessa held back the tears, because her own father had ratted her out to the man who was harming her. "My father didn't want me to divorce Bradley."

"Why?" Drake asked once he finally relaxed. His expression turned from anger to worry.

"I really don't know," she answered, shaking her head. "He just tried to tell me everything was going to be okay and I needed to stay with him, because he didn't want me to go through what my parents went through when they divorced."

"Divorce is so common with humans," Gunner snarled. "I really don't understand how you cannot find a true mate amongst yourselves."

"Some do find their mates," Tessa offered. "Mine just wasn't with the man I thought. He told me all the things I wanted to hear, and I fell for it."

"I assure you, Tessa," Rex nodded toward Drake, "we are bound by our paranormal nature. If his bear has claimed you, you were chosen by Mother Nature herself to be mated to my brother."

Why did she believe him?

"I need a moment," she said in a rush, standing up from her seat. All three men stood as she pushed her chair back in and ran toward Drake's room. She locked herself in the bathroom.

Tessa wiped away tears, kicking herself mentally for letting Rex's words freak her out. Drake's claim was valid. The shifters *were* different. Hell, everyone knew that. She hadn't really paid much attention to the news of their discovery, because she had been too busy running away from Bradley.

What little she'd read online was more speculation than truth. Tessa didn't blame them. She wouldn't want to be studied either.

"Tessa," Drake called out as he knocked softly on the door. "What's wrong, little one?"

"I'm sorry," she sniffled as she opened the door. She walked out and took a seat on the edge of his bed. "I'm just a little overwhelmed by everything you and your brothers are saying to me."

"About you being my mate?" he asked, taking her chin with the back of his index finger. He only gave her a nudge, but she knew to look into his eyes.

There was worry mixed with passion in his eyes. The dark-brown depths flickered gold as he released her to use his thumb to wipe away a lone tear that escaped her left eye. Once he was satisfied her face was void of tears, he returned his finger to the spot under her chin.

"He was a dominant male, correct?" Drake asked, his voice steady and sure.

"Yes, Sir," she replied in a whisper.

"He didn't respect you or your limits?" he continued. Tessa felt tears in her eyes again, but they didn't fall over her lashes this time. Drake's strength was enough for her to straighten her spine and continue to answer his questions.

"No, he did not," she sighed. "He got off on my fear."

"Did he strike you every time?"

"Yes," she flinched, remembering the nights she'd be cowered in the corner of the kitchen as he took a belt to her body.

Drake growled, "Where did he strike you?"

"There wasn't a spot he didn't use the belt on me," she admitted, still looking into his eyes.

"I want you to tell me exactly what he did to you so that when I find him, I can return every strike to him before I take his life," Drake promised.

"My feet, legs, ass," she paused to take a deep breath, "my breasts, my face…everywhere, Drake."

"Thank you for trusting me with your past, Tessa," Drake whispered, and released her. "Come here."

Tessa stood, trusting Drake as he pulled her close. He used his large hand to cup the back of her head. He didn't hesitate as he brought her head to his chest. "Tessa, I vow to you, I will always take care of you, and at no time will I ever raise a hand to you in anger. Everything I have told you about my kind has been nothing but the truth. It took one touch to know you were to be mine, and I will protect you, even if that means laying my life down for yours."

"Oh, Drake," she cried. "Where have you been all this time?"

"Waiting for you," he said, ducking his head to capture her lips.

The beast inside him roared so loudly, Drake couldn't hear his own thoughts over the bear. It was a victory for all three of them; Tessa finally trusted him, he finally trusted her, and his bear finally felt at peace knowing his mate had been found.

Tessa kissed him with the passion of a million lovers. Her lips were as soft as the wings of a butterfly, and the scent of honeysuckle that came from her skin was the potion that called to him. He wanted this little human, and every bit of past tragedy that came along with her.

"If you tell me to stop, I will stop," he said, touching the side of her face. He slid his hand around the back of her neck and ran his thumb over her bottom lip. He kissed her again after moving his thumb down the center of her neck. She remained still as he memorized the feel of her skin against his palm. Oh, how he wanted to take her tonight, but he wouldn't. She wasn't ready for a mating. As bad as he ached to mount her, he would wait.

"I don't know if I want you to stop," she swallowed.

"I will have you, but today will not be the day," he replied.

"Drake…" She let her words fall off as he kissed her once again.

"We will go for a walk in the woods," he announced as he released her. Tessa swayed for a second where she stood but corrected herself and opened her eyes. The haze of desire was easy to see in them. "My beast needs to roam."

"Okay," she breathed.

"Come, little one," he ordered. She took his hand as they emerged from the hallway leading to his room. Rex and Gunner had left when he got up from the table to check on her after a few minutes.

Her plate was still on the table, and Drake pointed at it. "Finish eating."

She nodded and sat down. He busied himself with cleaning up the leftovers and washing dishes. He didn't want to crowd Tessa. She'd already brought up too many emotions from her past, and tonight was supposed to be about them getting out for a stroll.

Tessa obviously liked his bear and was genuinely curious. He looked over his shoulder and stared at the back of her head for a moment. He still couldn't believe she was human…and a good one at that.

She finished her wine and set her fork and knife on the plate before standing up to come over to the sink. "Let me clean the dishes."

"I've got it." He smiled and took the plates, scrubbing them off and adding them to the dishwasher. "Go on out to the back porch, and I'll be right there."

Tessa left out the door, and Drake's bear

prowled in his mind. He was ready to show Tessa the wooded land behind his home. It wanted her to be happy here, and he wanted to provide everything her heart desired.

"Down, boy," Drake mumbled as he wiped his hands.

He kicked off his boots by the door and walked out onto the wooden porch. Tessa sat on the top step that led down to the yard. There was a cool breeze on the air since the sun had set. The moon was just starting to cast a glow across the backyard.

"It's dark in the woods," Tessa observed as she looked out toward a trail he and his brothers used to enter the forest behind his home.

Drake frowned. "I forget your eyesight isn't like ours."

"What do you mean?" she asked.

"We have enhanced vision and sense of smell," he offered. "In my bear form, I can see at night as if it were day."

"Do you have a flashlight for me?"

"No need for that," he smiled. "You can climb on my back while we go for a walk."

"What?"

"You heard me." He winked and removed his shirt. He didn't miss the blush on her pale cheeks when her eyes roamed his broad chest. He unbuckled his belt and the top button of his jeans before she turned away. He dropped his pants and removed his socks the moment his bear pushed for release.

The change was fast, only taking a few seconds for his body to shift. The beast shook its head and huffed to get her attention. When she looked at him, the bear laid down on its belly at her feet.

"I can't believe you want me to do this," she laughed, and the sound was beautiful.

The bear huffed and used his long nose to nudge her hand. Drake's human mind encouraged her to climb on, willing her to hear him. He didn't think she'd be this apprehensive since she'd been so forthcoming with her questions.

"Fine, but you better not run through the woods and let me fall off, Drake's bear," she huffed, and threw her leg over his back. The bear made a sound of contentment and waited until she was fully seated to begin walking toward the woods.

Tessa leaned forward and laid against his back, drawing her feet up on the bear's back. If Drake thought she was small before, feeling her on his back made her the tiniest human he'd ever seen. He continued to walk as she rested the side of her face against the back of his neck.

The sound of his paws crunching over dead leaves from the winter were the only sounds around them. Any small animal that might be around would've run away already from the scent of his bear.

It was so early in the spring, the bugs and frogs who sang at night were still quiet.

He knew a spot he wanted to show her on his land. It was one he hoped she'd enjoy. Their home only sat on twenty acres of land to the west of their crops, but unlike the fields, their personal land was covered with trees. The only spot it was open was a small meadow next to a pond not far from his home.

"Oh, this is beautiful," she gasped softly as they came into the clearing. The moon was illuminating the water, and Tessa dropped off the bear's back to get a closer look. "It looks like glass."

There was no breeze tonight, and the pond appeared that way with the moon shining off the water. The bear walked to the edge and dipped his front paws in, raking one across the water to splash Tessa. She yelped and jumped back but began laughing when she realized what he was doing.

"How much of Drake is still in there?" she wondered aloud, reaching over to run her fingers through the thick fur on top of his head. Drake's beast rumbled when she twirled her fingers around the top of his left ear. "I wish we could speak when you're in this form."

Drake's bear didn't make any acknowledgements other than a gentle nod. Tessa watched him as he prowled over to a spot to their right by a clump of trees. He huffed as he laid on his side, telling his mate to come closer. Tessa stared into his eyes for a moment, and the bear made a jerking motion with its head before she did as she was told. He used his paw to pull her against his chest, and his female melted against him.

"This is a beautiful spot," she said.

They both grew quiet as she tucked her hand under her head. With the other hand, Tessa picked at a few brown leaves on the ground.

"I don't want to run anymore," she said after several minutes. "I like it here."

Drake's bear huffed in response. Drake stopped it from snarling loudly at the thought of her leaving. The last thing he wanted to do was scare her even more. The male she'd been married to would pay for all the things he'd done to her. No dominant male should ever abuse their mate.

"Can we go back to the house now?" she asked, blinking as if she were trying to stay awake.

Drake's bear nudged her side, indicating she should climb on his back. The moment she settled in, he began walking. The beast occasionally tested the air for scents, always protecting his mate. He would sense danger before it arrived, and he was ready to defend Tessa if the time came.

The walk back was quiet, and for a bit of time, Drake was sure she'd fallen asleep on his back. By the time they reached the house, Rex and Gunner were sitting on the back porch. Both males stood up to walk toward the steps. He saw the happiness in his brothers' eyes as they watched Tessa and Drake together.

Something about Tessa softened his heart toward her kind. He couldn't say that it was because she was a female. All shifters had special places in their hearts for them, but he truly thought it was Tessa's aura and selflessness that called to them. She had a heart of gold.

Drake stopped, allowing Tessa to slide off his back. He commanded his bear to return to his mind, and the shift began. Within seconds, he was human and his mate turned toward the house while he pulled on his jeans.

"We are heading to the bar," Rex announced, walking toward Drake. As he approached, Drake noticed his softness change into something harder, fiercer. "Going to take a look around town. I don't trust this male."

"It's important that I get with that sheriff," Drake growled as he watched Tessa take a seat in a rocking chair on the back porch. He needed to find her ex-husband and kill him.

"I'll see if he's around tonight," Rex replied, hooking his thumb over his shoulder. "Go spend some time with your mate. We have to work the fields tomorrow."

"Who is going to watch Tessa?" Drake panicked.

"No one will come on our lands," Rex promised.

"We've been seen with her at the diner," Drake argued, running his hand over the top of his head. "I don't want her alone."

"She has to work tomorrow. I'm sure Gaia is more than capable of keeping Tessa safe," Rex pointed out.

"I'd still like someone else there," Drake said. He didn't want to leave her unprotected. Even with Gaia there, this male could do harm. "I'll make a call to the cats."

"Drive her to and from work tomorrow and talk to the Shaw pride. I'll find Sheriff Lynch."

Drake shook his brother's hand and watched as he entered the house to yell for Gunner. The two of them said their goodbyes to Tessa and walked around the side of the house to Rex's truck. A few seconds later, he heard the two doors open and close before Rex started the truck and left their land.

He had Tessa to himself for the night, but she looked exhausted. As he held out his hand for her, she looked up at him with a softness that cracked his hardened heart. She was human, but perfect for him. He couldn't hate her for the species she was born in to or blame her for the death of his parents.

No, Tessa was perfect for him.

"Are you ready for bed?"

"Please," she yawned, making a soft sound as she covered her mouth. "I have to get up early for work tomorrow."

"I will drive you to work, but I won't be able to stay," he stated. "We must get the seeds in the ground in the next few weeks, and we are already behind."

"Okay," she frowned. "That's fine. I can drive myself, but I need to get my car."

"No," he shook his head, "I will drive you to and from work until we find him. Gaia knows how to get in touch with me if something happens."

Tessa nodded and walked ahead of him. He couldn't help but watch the swing of her hips as she walked inside his home. She turned left down the first hallway off the living room and made her way into his living space.

"Drake?" She paused to turn around. "May I ask you a question?"

"Yes," he chuckled. Tessa was full of questions. Why was she being so shy now?

"Will…will you sleep in the bed with me?" she blushed. "I mean, you don't have to if you don't want to. I…I just like having you close."

"You do, huh?" he drawled. God damn, could he actually sleep next to her without wanting to mount his mate? Probably not.

"I'd like it if you did," she confirmed.

"Get your shower," he told her. "I'll be in here waiting for you when you come out."

"Thank you."

Drake turned down the bed and fluffed the pillows. He removed his jeans and donned a pair of basketball shorts while she showered. His bear growled in his mind, demanding he follow Tessa into the bathroom to bathe her, but he pushed at his beast, commanding it to stand down.

There would be time for them to be together if she accepted him. He would never force her to do anything she didn't want to do, and even if that meant he was alone forever, he'd let her go.

Maybe?

Maybe not…

The thought of Tessa leaving sent his fangs through his gums. Drake took a deep breath and calmed his other side, hoping he wouldn't be half-shifted by the time she emerged from the bathroom.

Damn, his beast was persistent, demanding he mark her so no other males would come near her. He couldn't bite her tonight. That would have to wait until their mating night. He could, however, hold her while she slept, ensuring his scent would be on her while she worked for most of the day tomorrow.

The water shut off and Tessa opened the door after several minutes. The light from the bathroom sent a halo around her body as she paused in the doorway. His cock hardened as she stood there, wearing a tank top and some tiny, cotton shorts. The matching outfit was covered in bright pink flowers on a black background, and he inhaled when her natural scent of honeysuckle reached his nose.

"Ready for bed?" he asked, turning on his side.

"Yes," she yawned again, climbing in the bed. Drake watched as she nestled into the pillows he'd put on the side of the bed closest to the bathroom. Tessa let out a soft sigh when she found the spot she needed to be comfortable.

He turned off the light on the nightstand and pulled the covers over his shoulder, closing his eyes and letting sleep take him as soon as he heard her breathing even out. His mate was safe and sound in his home, and he could finally rest.

Chapter 9

Gaia smiled widely when Tessa entered the diner. Today was going to be another short day for her. It was five-thirty in the morning, and Drake had dropped her off at the door with a promise to be back fifteen minutes before noon to pick her up.

"What are you so happy about?" Tessa asked her boss as she made her way toward the breakroom where her apron hung on a peg behind the door.

"So, how did it go with Drake Morgan?" Gaia asked with a raised brow. Tessa was glad the diner was closed, because she wanted to ask questions about the Morgan family.

"Everything was fine," Tessa hedged. Gaia's emerald green eyes sparkled for a moment before she righted her features.

"He and his brothers are good men, Tessa," Gaia stated with a hearty nod. "Treat them kindly. They've been through a lot."

"Are you like them?" Tessa asked, tying the strings of her apron together at her back. "Like the Morgans?"

"Ah, no," Gaia shook her head, "I am not."

"So, you know?" Tessa pressed. Gaia was

keeping something from her, and she wanted to know what it was. Her boss looked away for several seconds before righting her features to look into Tessa's eyes.

"We do not speak of that around here," Gaia scolded. "Tony is here, and we need to get the food prepped."

"Yes, ma'am." Tessa was about to say something about Tony not being in the building when she heard the cook's loud truck pull into the lot. Whatever Gaia knew, she didn't want it talked about in her diner.

The diner opened at six, and the early morning patrons came in to get their coffee and breakfast. Usually, it was the older generation. Retired men would come in and meet up once or twice a week for a meal. That morning, three large men with bright blue eyes entered when the doors opened. Gaia met them at the door, and they all headed to the same table in the back corner where Drake and Rex had sat the day before.

"Who are those men?" Tessa asked Gaia as she rounded up cups and a carafe full of fresh coffee.

"Those are the Shaw pride's Guardians," Gaia whispered. "It seems they owed Drake a favor, and he called it in."

"A favor?" she frowned. "To watch over me?"

"That's my understanding." Gaia shrugged and

balanced the tray on her palm. "Can you brew another pot of coffee?"

Tessa busied herself with making coffee and taking orders at the bar by the register. As soon as she served the men there, she made her way around to a new couple who had just sat down by the door.

Tessa wondered what Drake had done for them in the past that warranted sending three huge men into the diner to sit half the day and watch over her. Drake wanted to be at the diner, but with it being time to work in the fields, she wanted him to put his business first, regardless of how he spoke of the way shifters took care of their mates in all things.

The diner slowed down enough for Tessa to take another pot of coffee over to the men's table. As she approached, she noticed they were not only large, but extremely handsome. The one who sat on the left side of the table was the largest of the bunch, with curly, brown hair and a sneer on his face that could rival Drake's. The other two were not much smaller than the first. The one across from the largest man was blond, and his blue eyes stood out against his tanned skin. The other one was younger and dressed as if he was going to a play a round of golf. He wore slacks and a short-sleeved polo that tested the limits of the seams with his ginormous muscles.

"Good morning." She smiled as she approached. "I understand that Drake asked you to be here?"

"Yes," the blond one said. "My name is Winter, and this is Noah and Savage."

Savage was the largest one, and his name fit him. The three men nodded in her direction but didn't reach out to shake her hand. She was about to offer hers when she remembered Drake talking about pain from another male's touch, and that was something she didn't want to experience.

"I'm sorry you were called away from whatever you were doing to come sit here for half of the day," Tessa apologized.

"Drake needed us," Savage began, swirling his finger around the air in front of him. "We honor our favors, and if Drake needs help, we know it's important."

"Thank you," she replied.

The men tucked into their food while she busied herself with cleaning off two tables by the door. It was quiet in the diner, and she was glad to have a bit of a reprieve. Without Drake around, she felt a little uneasy every time the door opened, but knowing the panthers were there made it a little easier.

"God damn, Drake," Rex barked as he jumped off the plow. "What the hell is wrong with you?"

"Nothing," Drake grumped.

"You really need to officially mate Tessa," Gunner complained as he threw his lunchbox in the back of the truck. "You are a fucking asshole without her."

They'd been in the field for the entire morning, and Drake was about to leave to get Tessa when something set him off about the way Rex was running the plow. He'd yelled at him over the two-way radio, causing his middle brother to stop work and give him an ass chewing face to face.

"It's too soon," Drake snapped. "I really don't need you to tell me when I should approach the subject with her."

"You haven't told her?" Rex roared, his brother's eyes flashing a golden glow. "Really, Drake?"

"I've told her that we mate, but I haven't quite gotten to the details yet," he mumbled, taking off his old trucker hat and slapping it against the top of his thigh to knock off the dust.

"You need to take care of that tonight, brother," Rex barked. "Don't come to this field tomorrow and yell at me again, because I won't put up with your shit."

Drake felt his beast rumble behind his skin. He had to force it back where it belonged. Rex wasn't his enemy. "I'm going to get Tessa."

"See you at home," Rex said through gritted teeth. Their little tiff wasn't going to break them. Drake couldn't remember how many times they'd tussled in the backyard after an argument. They fought their battles like the animals they were, and Drake had a few scars on his human skin to show for it.

Drake left the fields and headed north to town. As he passed the field Gunner had planted the day before, he looked over and took note that everything looked as it should. They had a few more weeks of work before they would be done. He planned on making sure Tessa was protected during that time. He didn't know if he could ask the panthers to watch her for that long, but if he had to, he would stay with her and trust his brothers to get the fields ready.

His main concern was Tessa. The human female had weaved a web around his heart. Her ex-husband was in town, and no one knew where he was. He had some connections over the state line in Memphis, Tennessee, but those were a last resort if he was unable to defend his home. Rex and Gunner were well equipped to take care of the male as soon as he was found.

And he would be found.

He saw Tessa through the window of the diner. She was laughing and talking to a customer as she refilled their drink. Drake didn't move for a few minutes, just watched her as she worked. The female inside the diner was his. His nature had proved it to him the moment he'd touched her when she stumbled and fell at his feet. It was as if the goddess herself knew what he wanted…what he needed.

A customer coming out the door broke his train of thought, and Drake turned off his truck to go inside to get Tessa. The moment he entered, Savage, Winter, and Noah stood up to shake his hand.

"I appreciate you being here," he stated.

"Everything went well," Savage told him. "We are offering the pride's services in finding this asshole so you can put him down."

"You are going to put him down, right?" Winter pressed.

"As soon as I can find this son of a bitch," Drake paused to check for anyone within hearing range and continued when he found none, "I will deal out the punishment of our kind."

"I hope it is as brutal as our own," Savage sneered.

"I guarantee it," Drake promised.

"We will send over three other Guardians tomorrow," Savage offered.

"I can't ask that of you," Drake said as he

waved his hand.

"Why?" Winter chuckled. "Because we only asked you to come hang at *The Deuce* twice?"

"Yeah," Drake replied, looking up at the males. They were worthy of their titles as Guardians of the Shaw pride. These men were the best of their kind, and not only for their strength, but for their compassion toward others. "I cannot ask this of you."

"Well, you don't have to ask," Noah said. "We are offering our services with no need for repayment."

"That's very kind of you," Drake sighed. "I appreciate it, but I think I will be keeping Tessa at home until this is over."

All three males chuckled and looked over his shoulder. Savage was the first to shake his head, sobering when he jutted his chin out toward Tessa as she was coming out of the backroom of the diner. "That female of yours doesn't like to sit still. I can advise you after having found my mate, they are strong-willed, and I wouldn't put it past that one to disagree with you holding her hostage."

"Why am I being held hostage?" Tessa asked as she approached, overhearing Savage's statement.

"I think it would be best if you stay home for the next few days," Drake stated, wrapping an arm around her waist as she frowned. "It's safer that way."

"I have to work, Drake," she said through clenched teeth. "We've discussed this."

"Then you work for me this week, and I'll pay you twice what you are making here," he stated. He would pay her three or four times what she made if it kept her out of town and away from her apartment and her ex-husband.

Tessa quieted, her expressive blue eyes tracing his face. The other males made their excuses to leave, and she righted her features long enough to tell them goodbye. As the panthers left the diner, she finally closed her eyes. With a heavy sigh, she said, "If you want me to stay home, we need to talk to Gaia. I can't just leave her here alone."

"I'll talk to Gaia," he promised, seeing the owner across the room. It only took a nod from her to give him his answer. Gaia wanted Tessa safe, too. "It is done. Let's go."

"Wait? What's done?" Tessa asked, confused. "Drake? What's going on?"

"I'll explain at home," he grunted. "We need to go."

"Fine," she huffed, but accepted his hand as they left the diner. He would take her home, feed her lunch, and like his brothers suggested, tell her everything.

It was time to officially mate Tessa Ward.

Chapter 10

Drake entered his home and immediately went to work preparing his mate something to eat. Tessa sat down at the kitchen table and turned in her seat so she could watch him. He kept an eye on her through his periphery and groaned under his breath when she removed the elastic band from her hair, letting it fall free around her face. She ran her fingers through it and pulled it over to one side. Her long, blonde locks curled ever so slightly, and he wanted to tangle his fingers in them to hold her tight so he could capture her lips again.

"Tell me what you like on your sandwich," he mumbled around his sharp fangs. The need to bite her and mark her was overwhelming. His beast was demanding he forgo food and mount her, but he forced it down and waited for her reply.

"Mustard, lettuce, and tomato is fine," she answered, patiently waiting for Drake to sit down with her. He could see the questions in her eyes and was surprised she was waiting before unleashing them.

"Go ahead and eat," he ordered, setting the plate in front of her before returning to the counter to make his own. He slapped his together quickly and sat down at the head of the table. Tessa was on his right, exactly where he wanted her.

"What's going on?" she asked. "I feel like there's something you need to tell me."

"Rex and Gunner searched the town last night," he admitted. "They couldn't find him, nor has anyone seen him."

"I know it was him, Drake," she growled, impressing him at how his sweet mate turned aggressive when speaking about the enemy.

"I don't doubt you, Tessa," Drake assured her, reaching over to touch her hand. His bear pushed at his human skin when the connection of its mate was felt. "Finish eating and we will go for a walk."

"Okay," she said, accepting his offer.

It took them only a few more minutes to clean up, and Tessa excused herself to the bathroom. When she returned, she'd already changed out of her jeans and work shirt, donning a pair of black track pants and a white cotton shirt. She wore a pair of tennis shoes, and Drake smiled as he led her out to the porch.

"You're not shifting?" she asked.

"No, we are going to talk about my world as we take our walk," he replied, and took he hand as he continued down the stairs leading off the back porch.

"What else do you need to tell me?"

The shade of the trees in the woods behind his home sent a cool chill through the air. Tessa shivered and Drake pulled her closer, offering his body for warmth. When she relaxed, he stopped and took her face with his right hand, never letting go of his connection.

The kiss was soft, passionate, and full of need. He wanted her to know she was going to be his. When her hands fisted in his shirt, he deepened the kiss. Her tongue was soft as velvet, and his chest rumbled, telling her he wanted her. He didn't know if she could sense his need like a female bear could, but he found his answer when Tessa pressed her body closer to his.

"Drake…" she whispered, then accepted another heated kiss. His body hardened, priming itself for the mating that needed to be done.

"Tell me you'll be my mate," he urged. "My beast wants to mark you as my own."

"Mark me?" she questioned when he released her lips.

"I need to tell you what will happen if you say yes," he groaned. "Let's walk."

She hesitated. "Why are we going into the woods, Drake?"

"Because, you are more at peace here," he replied. "I've noticed how much you like it, and I want you to be at ease when I tell you about how my kind mates."

"Oh," she blushed. "Well, you can tell me. I need to know, but I think I already know."

"Have you been on the human's internet again?" he teased. She was quite inquisitive.

"There was an article," she admitted. "It said there were bite scars on some of the female's necks."

"This is true," he growled. "The scientists got more information than we previously thought."

"I'm sorry," she said, resting a hand over his heart. "I'm so sorry for the way humans have treated the shifters. I hate them for capturing you as if you were the worst kind of animals."

"Where have you been all my life?" he asked, capturing her lips again.

"Tell me what I need to do, Drake," she pressed as soon as he released her to take a breath. If Drake had his way, he'd never stop kissing Tessa. "What do I need to do to become your mate?"

"We bite our mates, and the bite will scar over to show other males not to come near, or even touch, a mated female." Drake held nothing back. Tessa had to know everything. Yes, there was a risk she would run from him and tell the humans everything, but he was willing to take that risk and hope she accepted him.

"But I can't bite you," she said, reaching up to touch her own teeth. "I don't have fangs like a female of your kind would have."

"Oh, Tessa," he flinched. "There is always a way."

"How?" she continued. "Tell me."

"I can always change you into what I am," he offered, watching as her eyes widened. The one thing he didn't want to do was scare her, but the look of shock on her face proved he may have done just that.

"Really?" she asked, clearing her throat.

"It's not easy," he replied, swallowing hard at the thought. "It's painful."

"How painful?"

"Like someone is breaking all of your bones over and over again for three days while you transform into one of us," he admitted. "I will have to be sedated, because once I mark you and give you my blood, we are bonded for eternity. Your pain will be my pain, and your agony will be mine, as well."

"Is there medicine that can sedate me, too?" she cringed. "I've had broken bones, Drake, and I don't like what you're saying...what you're suggesting."

"The last thing I want to do is put you in any type of pain," he growled. "I would rather cut off my own arms and bleed out on the ground."

"Is there a medicine, Drake?" she pressed.

"Yes," he nodded, "but it's not very effective. You'll still feel pain."

"Okay," she said, quieting as she released his

hand.

The bear inside him roared, demanding he go after her when she walked ahead of him. She didn't want this. She didn't want to be his. The anger boiled up inside him. This was why humans were no good for them.

"Tessa?" he called out, taking a step forward, but paused when she spun around. Her arms were crossed over her chest like she was protecting herself. She was scared, and he could scent the fear on the breeze.

"I want you to do it," she stated. "If it means I can be as strong as you and your brothers, I want in."

"What?"

"I don't understand all of these feelings I'm having when I'm around you, Drake, but my heart is telling me that everything you're telling me is true."

"It's all true," he promised, taking three large steps to grab ahold of his mate.

"Then mate me, Drake Morgan," she breathed as his lips crashed down on hers.

"I'm demanding," he warned.

"And grumpy," she added as he scooped her up in his arms.

"I like control," he continued. "And I know you only want that inside the bedroom. I accept that fully."

"I faithfully give you control over me, but only

when I am on my knees before you," she vowed, resting her forehead against the crook of his neck. Her fingers tangled in his long, corkscrew curls as he marched toward his home…their home. Tessa was finally going to be his.

He didn't set her down until they entered his room. The need inside his body was a full-on raging inferno. It'd been a long time since he had a woman in his bed, but this was different. This was his mating.

"Undress," he ordered. "I want to see what's mine."

Tessa kicked off her shoes and socks, standing from the bed to remove her top. Drake's eyes roamed her body as she shimmied out of her track pants. She wore a white lace bra with matching panties. The bra cupped her breasts enough for them to swell over the material. He wanted nothing more than to use his claws to shred them, but he wouldn't. He wanted her to prove she was willing to give him every part of herself.

Tessa didn't hesitate as she unhooked her bra, sliding the straps down her arms. She bent at the waist and removed her panties, standing up straight to hold them out to the side before letting go. The sheer material drifted to the floor with the weight of a feather.

"Beautiful," he said in awe.

"Thank you…Sir," she replied, taking a knee.

She was slow on her descent, but when her second knee landed, he knew she was destined to be his. Drake's heart burst open when she rested on the back of her legs.

Drake removed his shirt and walked to Tessa's left side, resting his hand on her shoulder "What are your hard limits?"

"No belts." She paused to take a deep breath. Drake knew she was reliving her time with Bradley, and he was going to do everything in his power to wipe that motherfucker from her mind. "No fists...of any kind. No fire. No blades."

"What are you safewords?" he continued, taking a moment to run his big palm over her soft hair. He wanted to braid it for their mating. It was long enough he could still wrap it around his hand as he mounted her from behind.

"Red, yellow, green," she stated, not moving from her place. It broke his heart that she had that training, not from a good Dom, but from years of abuse.

"I want to braid your hair," he told her. On her nod, Drake laid his palm on top of her head, directing her to bow. She complied without complaint and waited patiently for him to twist the hair as he preferred. He kept a hair tie on his side table for his own hair and used that to bind the ends of her braid.

"Are you wet for me already, Tessa?" he asked

as he finished. Drake used his index finger to lift her face, and what he saw there undid him.

Trust.

"Yes, Sir," she smiled.

Drake held out his hand and waited for Tessa to take it. When she did, he helped her to her feet and spun her around so quickly, she gasped.

"Bend over the bed," he ordered as he pressed his palm to the spot between her shoulder blades. Tessa moaned so lightly she probably didn't think he noticed, but he did, and the sound was like music to his ears.

Drake knelt behind her and ran his hand over her thighs. Her pussy was right at mouth level, and the sight before him made his mouth water. He tightened his hold on her hips and ran his tongue over her clit, stopping to nibble at her folds. "I've had one taste, and I'm already addicted."

Tessa's thighs quivered with each slow pass of his tongue. Her moans of pleasure increased as he continued. Her breathing increased, and he released her, smiling when she let out a vicious curse.

"On your back, mate," he ordered.

Tessa climbed on the bed and rested her head on one the pillows. Drake removed his jeans and joined her. She groaned out in frustration when he laid down next to her. A smirk formed on his lips when she closed her eyes. "I will mount you when you are primed for me."

"Yes, Sir," she breathed out.

Drake kissed her hard, his hand sliding between her legs. His fingers danced across her pussy, pulling back when she lifted her hips in a silent plea for release.

"The more you demand of me, the slower I will go," he warned.

Tessa nodded and squinted her eyes. She was trying, and he loved watching her need build. The blush to her pale cheeks mesmerized him. He wanted to taste every inch of her body. It didn't matter if he took all night to find his release. Making sure Tessa was satisfied was his top priority.

"Touch me, Tessa," he ordered.

"Do you like that?" Drake's eyes roamed Tessa's body. Her nipples were tight, pink buds, and he grasped the outside of one of her thick thighs. He knew he should just give her what she wanted, but making his mate squirm from the delayed satisfaction turned him on. He was a patient man when it came right down to it and could hold out for a while. Oh, he would eventually satisfy her, but for now, she would have to wait for release.

"Yes, yes, I do, Sir," she whimpered.

"I've waited forever to find you, my mate."

Drake climbed between her legs and Tessa wrapped her arms around his neck. Their eyes were on each other as he pushed his cock against her. The moment they connected, he felt his world right itself. He moved slowly, allowing her to adjust to him. Tessa threw her legs over his hips and accepted the kiss he gave her as he increased his thrusts.

"You cannot come until I bite you," he ordered.

"Yes, Sir," she answered with a smile, and those two words were all he needed to hear.

He'd found his true mate, and she was everything he'd hoped she would be.

There was only one man she'd kneel before, and he was a deadly beast capable of killing her. Drake's body swelled as he covered her during their love-making. He said he was dominant, but he was also a patient lover. Maybe with time he would change? Like Bradley had?

No, she couldn't think that way. Drake was different. He was a shifter, and shifters were loyal and loving. Even at the diner, the panthers had told her the same thing. The way they talked about their mates and their children was a testament to their love for their forever mate.

Forever mate.

She wanted to test the saying on her tongue, but she wouldn't do it while Drake was around. Especially while he was buried deep inside her.

"Tessa," he growled. "Don't think. Just feel, little one."

"Yes, Sir," she replied, shaking all thoughts from her mind.

Tessa felt her body relax the moment Drake wrapped his huge hand around her neck. There was no pressure against the column of her throat until he slid his hand up to her jaw in a dominant hold. The movement held her face immobile, and she felt the stirrings of an orgasm waiting on the wings of his next move. Even with this dominant hold he had over her, she trusted Drake with everything she had.

Drake's eyes flashed gold as his beast made itself known, and he slid from her body. His mouth opened and fangs grew from where his human teeth once were. The sight before her was raw and wild. She panted hard, feeling his cock where it laid heavily against the inside of her thigh. All she had to do was shift, and he'd slide right into her pussy again…right where she wanted him…right where she needed him.

"You are mine now, Tessa," he growled, his voice thickening with each word. "I'm going to mount you from behind and bite your neck to mark you. If you're going to stop me, now would be the time."

"Do it, Drake," she panted, still unable to move her head. "Make me yours."

He released her, his hands working fast to push her over to her belly. Those large hands of his grasped her hips and lifted her ass into the air. She knew better than to move, and she was right. Drake's hand wrapped around the braid in her hair as he slid his thick cock back into her. The change of position bubbled her orgasm to the brink.

"I need to come," she begged on a soft breath.

"You will when I mark you," he growled as he pulled her upright on the bed. She was on her knees facing away from him as he pounded into her body. Oh, god, she needed him so bad.

"Do it," she begged. "Please?"

A snarl echoed in the room as he tilted her head to the side. The strike of his teeth into the spot where her neck and shoulders met sent her into a release so intense, all she could do was whimper. It didn't matter. Drake knew what he was doing as he gave her everything she needed.

Tessa closed her eyes and let the orgasm consume her. Drake's punishing thrusts fed her need to be taken. She smiled into the darkness as he slowed, finally coming to a stop when his own release subsided.

He lowered her to the mattress and curled his body around her, pulling just a thin sheet over their bodies. He kissed the spot on her neck where he'd bitten her, and she hummed her contentment.

"You okay?" he whispered against her ear. At no time had he let go of her hair or the hold he had on her hip. The left side of her neck throbbed from his bite, but it subsided the moment he made a pass over it with his tongue.

"I'm good," she sighed, going limp in his arms. There was no way she could move after a that. "Tired."

"We will sleep," he promised, helping her to lay on her side. He spooned up behind her and kissed the spot where he'd just bitten her. "It's healed already, but the scar remains, Tessa."

"That means we are forever mates?" she asked, finally hearing the words from her own lips. She liked the sound of it.

"Yes, Tessa," he breathed against her skin. "If we were not, the bite would've vanished after it healed."

"So, I'm yours?" she asked, needing to hear it one more time.

"Yes, Tessa…You are mine."

Chapter 11

The next morning, Tessa looked in the bathroom mirror and pressed her fingers to the spot on her neck. There were two scars, but no scabs. The marks looked like they were months old inside of eight hours.

"My saliva healed it," Drake spoke as he entered the bathroom. Tessa looked at him through the mirror. Drake was shirtless, but wore his denim jeans. Her eyes roamed his chest and traveled up to his eyes. "The scar tells other males you are mine."

"I remember you saying that." She paused to turn around. Drake took her hands into his as she approached, leaning down to kiss her softly.

"What's wrong?"

"Are you going to change me into what you are?" she asked.

"I don't want you to be in pain," he said, releasing her hand to stroke her cheek. "I also want you to be sure."

"Do *you* want me to be like you?" she pushed, capturing his hand as he continued to touch her skin.

The connection was stronger. She could feel the electricity more so now that Drake had bitten her. He wasn't lying to her. Everything he'd promised was happening. Even the thought of being in pain to be with him was at the forefront of her mind, but it didn't matter. She wanted to change.

She wanted to be a beast like him.

"I want *you*, little one," Drake said as he closed his eyes tight. "I know I hated humans. Well, I still do, but you've changed me. I didn't know I'd find a mate outside of my kind."

"But do you want me to be a bear?" she continued. "I have to know, Drake."

"I want you to be like me, but it kills me to know you will be in pain," he cursed, wiping a hand over his face. Tessa could see the indecision in his expression.

"How bad will it be for you?" she asked.

"We will both survive," he answered.

"Drake," she growled, becoming agitated with his lack of answers. "You're skirting around what I'm asking you."

"I will be fine," he stated as he cleared his throat and grabbed a towel from the shelf behind the door. "I need to shower and get you to the diner."

"Okay," she softly said and dropped her head. He wasn't going to answer her.

Tessa busied herself as he stepped into the shower. The frosted glass hid him from her, but she could see his silhouette as he dipped his head under the spray. Oh, she wanted to undress and step in there with him, but she refrained.

She willed him to look at her…to talk to her, but he just pressed his palms to the cool tile and hung his head. *Please, look at me. Tell me something.*

"Tessa," he moaned, turning his head to the side. She couldn't see him looking at her through the glass, but she could feel his gaze, and it was intense. So much so, she touched the center of her chest as she waited for him to respond. "Please, go finish getting ready for work."

Tessa's breath rushed out of her lungs. His demand was followed by a rumbling from inside the shower. She wasn't afraid of Drake, but she knew if he and his bear were agitated, they felt strongly about whatever it was running through their minds.

She backed out of the bathroom and grabbed her shoes, sitting on the side of the bed to tie them. Drake emerged after several minutes and walked up to her before taking a knee at her feet.

"I will talk with a shifter doc today and get some answers on what we need to do to keep you comfortable," he promised. "My brothers will be here, too."

"For you or for me?" she asked.

"For both of us, because I don't know if I will be able to handle seeing you in pain without going insane."

"I don't want you to see me in pain if it will inflict pain on you, Drake," she worried.

"Let's get through our day, and I will have answers by dinner." He plastered on a smile, standing up to take her hand.

Tessa agreed with a nod and followed him out of his underground living quarters. Well, she guessed it'd be hers now too. She looked around the hallway as they made the slight incline toward the living room, and realized she liked being so tucked away.

"I could get used to this," she whispered, not realizing she'd said it loud enough for him to hear, when he stopped and turned around.

"Get used to what?" he asked, reaching back to take her hand. There was that connection again.

"Living here," she blushed.

"This is already yours, Tessa," he explained. "You are my forever mate."

"What about love, Drake?" she asked as soon as the thought popped in her head. Did she love this man? Maybe? Possibly?

"Our kind doesn't work quite the way humans do, Tessa," he said, leaning against the wall. He crossed his booted ankles, and she looked down at them when his spurs clinked at the action. God, she loved those spurs, and wouldn't mind if he wore them every single day. "We find our mates, and love follows."

"How do you know that you will fall in love with your mate?" she pressed, asking another twenty damned questions. Tessa couldn't help it…she was just curious.

"Because it always happens," he shrugged. "I've never met a couple who didn't fall in love."

She wouldn't admit it to him now, but she already had some major affection for him ever since he fed her that beef stew. He'd claimed to hate humans, had even been a major asshole to her, but when he realized she was hungry, the kind-hearted man he really was came out to provide for her. With Bradley showing up in town, and with Tulley calling in Drake to help Tessa out that night, she saw Drake Morgan for exactly who he was…passionate and caring. He loved his brothers, even if he wouldn't admit it, and he provided a home for them and their future mates.

"Come on, we're going to be late," he urged, and pushed away from the wall.

They left the house just as dark clouds were building in the skies toward town. She would be about five minutes late for work, but Drake assured her Gaia wouldn't mind.

When they pulled up, Gaia was already standing by the door to the diner. Tessa looked at the sky and ducked her head when she felt a raindrop hit her cheek. A rumble of thunder shook her spine as she stepped inside the diner. Her eyes landed on Gaia, and her boss looked relieved when they walked in the door. "I was getting a little worried about you."

"We had a delay," Tessa offered as a token of an excuse. "It won't happen again."

"Don't do that again," she scolded. "But if you do, a phone call would be nice."

"Gaia," Drake cleared his throat. "This was my fault. I had to talk to Tessa about something important this morning, and we were later than usual leaving my place."

"Understood," Gaia said, walking around the counter to start a pot of coffee. "Sit and let me make you some coffee, Drake. I'm sure this little rain cloud will disappear in a few minutes."

Tessa walked off to gather her things, and noticed her boss and Drake were talking quietly at the long bar by the kitchen. They didn't raise their voices, and Tessa was sure Gaia was worried for their safety and not really mad, but it did cause some unease seeing her boss act that way.

As she returned to the front of the diner, the clouds outside were gone with not a rain drop in sight and the sun was shining bright. Gaia smiled at Drake and walked away. A new customer came in and Tessa seated him at the end of the bar, as far away from Drake as possible.

The panthers entered only minutes later, taking

to the corner booth in the back of the room. Drake lazily slid off his stool. Those spurs of his clanked as he crossed the floor to greet them. Savage, Noah, and Winter all stood and shook his hand. The four men spoke for a minute and Drake turned to leave. Tessa jutted her chin out, indicating he should follow her to the backroom.

"I'll be here by noon again," he promised as she closed the door to the breakroom.

"Okay," she smiled. "If you need to, you can leave me at your place while you help your brothers."

"We are back on schedule," he offered. "If they need me, I will help them in the afternoons."

"I don't want to take you away from your business, Drake," she scowled, leaning against a small table that was pushed against the wall opposite the door.

"Both you and my crops are the most important things in my world." He smiled as he cupped her face. "Your safety and comfort comes first, regardless. If I have to spend a few extra days in the fields to get the seeds in the ground, it'll be okay."

"Promise me it's okay?"

"Promise, little one," he swore as he nodded and kissed her softly. The hairs from his short beard tickled her face, but she didn't complain.

"I'll see you later today, then," she whispered.

Drake left the diner after a brief chat with the Guardians from the Shaw pride. He wasn't going to the fields with his brothers like he'd told Tessa. Talon Shaw, the alpha of the pride, set up a meeting with the local sheriff at the werepanther-owned bar, *The Deuce*, before they opened. The lawman was already waiting for him to arrive.

As he parked and stepped out of his vehicle, the sheriff stood on the porch and waited for Drake to take the steps up before opening the door to let him in. Sheriff Lynch closed and locked the door behind them, taking a seat at the first table by the door.

"You wanted to see me?" he asked.

"I have a problem I need to take care of so my mate can live in peace," Drake explained. Talon reassured him anything Drake said to the lawman, when it came to the shifter world, he would understand.

"Tessa?" the sheriff asked.

"Yes, Tessa Ward."

"Go on."

Drake told him everything he knew, down to the male's name and where he'd last been seen. If the sheriff's office could keep an eye around town for Bradley, Drake would be forever grateful. There was only so much he and his brothers could do while planting crops and watching Tessa.

"I can do a little digging on him," Sheriff Lynch offered. "If he already has a record in the system, it'll be easier to keep tabs on him. Remember that if he doesn't show his face or get into trouble while he's lurking in the shadows, there's nothing I can do."

"I understand," Drake agreed. "Gaia is protecting the diner, and the cats have offered to be there for a few days for extra security."

"Gaia is capable of protecting Tessa," the sheriff snickered. "You don't trust her?"

"I trust her with my life," Drake replied. "I don't ask much of her, but she's taken it upon herself to protect Tessa and my family."

"I noticed the rainstorm the other day that came out of nowhere," Sheriff Lynch chuckled. "Who pissed her off?"

"That would be me," Drake said, quirking a brow at the lawman. Sheriff Garrett Lynch had his own tasks with watching the panthers. He wasn't here for the bears. The bears had their own goddess, but she wasn't their protector.

Gaia was more than an angel, and she was his bear clan's adopted godmother. Drake remembered the day his mother had sat him down to tell him about her boss at the diner.

"The earth is given to us temporarily. We must treat Mother Nature with respect, or she will take back what is owed to her, Drake."

Gaia could control the earth and the elements. She was Mother Nature in human form. His mother and father didn't know why she chose to come to this place and pretend to be human, but he was taught to never question her reasonings behind anything she did. Gaia knew what was best for everyone and everything.

"Glad you resolved that one," the sheriff chuckled as he leaned back in his chair. "I didn't want to have to deal with flooded roads or tornados."

"Agreed," Drake said, holding out his hand for the sheriff to shake. "You have my number. If you find anything, or see him, I want him brought to me."

"Shifter law will preside," the sheriff promised, tightening his hold on Drake's hand. "Take care of your mate."

"I plan on it," Drake said, releasing the male's hand.

As he left the bar, the breeze crossed his skin, and on the tail of it was trouble. Something was coming, and Drake didn't like what he felt. He knew Bradley was somewhere close, waiting for Tessa to be alone, and he refused to leave her without protection. When he found the male who had harmed his mate, he would kill him and make him suffer for everything he'd ever done to her.

The next stop was to the Shaw pride and their healer, Harold Blackwell. He was the only shifter doctor in the area, and he had what Drake needed to ensure Tessa was able to get through the change without being in too much pain.

As he pulled into the driveway, two Guardians exited the small security shack at the entrance. Since the humans discovered shifters, Talon Shaw had put up a fence and added guards to his land. Drake didn't blame him. There were too many people in his care that needed protection. Along with the Guardians, the werepanther pride held close to fifty shifters, and each one of them was loved and protected by the pride.

"What brings you by?" the Guardian, Ranger, asked as he rolled down his window. The large male leaned his elbow on the window ledge of Drake's truck and took a casual stance. A low rumble of thunder off in the distance had both males looking to the west.

"I need to speak with your healer," Drake announced. "I am in need of his services."

"Give me just a moment," Ranger said, lifting his cell phone from his pocket. He dialed up the healer and spoke to him quietly for a moment. Drake really didn't want to go into details as to why he was needing to see Harold, but he would if it got him through the gate. It was important he had the healer's medicine for his mate. "You can go on through. It's the first cottage on the left past the alpha's home."

"Much obliged." He nodded and drove through the gate when Ranger hit the button to open it.

As he drove up the long driveway, Drake noticed how the pride kept their land similar to his own. Trees covered up the view from the road and eventually opened into a clearing where the alpha's immaculate home resided. The driveway circled around to the left of the house, leading back into rows of cottages, all unique to their owners. The back yard was spacious, and a huge firepit was the main focal point. Across the backyard was a huge barn that appeared to have been renovated. Several cars and trucks parked in a small gravel lot behind it.

The healer's home was easy to find, and as soon as he pulled in, Harold stepped out onto the porch. He wore a pair of dark denim jeans and a black cotton shirt. His eyebrows narrowed as Drake exited the vehicle.

"Drake, what brings you by?" Harold asked. A beautiful female stepped out from behind Harold, but quickly stepped to the doc's back. From their body language, Drake assumed she was the healer's mate.

"I need to speak with you about changing a

human." He sighed. "I need your help."

"Please, come inside," Harold offered. "Luna, could you please bring us a couple of beers?"

"Sure." She smiled and disappeared inside the cottage.

"I didn't know you were mated," Drake stated.

"It's recent," Harold replied as a way of an answer. Drake scented the air and frowned. Luna wasn't a panther like the healer. Harold's eyes flashed an amber hue when he noticed Drake's actions. "She is a white wolf."

"A wolf?" Drake growled. Wolves were not good. They were feral and the worst kind of shifters. They caused death and destruction wherever they went, killing and maiming every shifter in their path. There was a code amongst shifters; all wolves were bad.

"A *white* wolf," Harold said, his chest swelling from the threat. Drake paused and looked past the healer.

"There's no such of a thing as a white wolf shifter," Drake growled.

"There is," Harold argued. "Luna is my mate, and I will protect her to the death. If you have a problem with her, then you best get in your truck and leave the property."

"I never said I had a problem with her," Drake sighed. "Look, I need your help. It isn't my business who your mate is as long as she is not feral."

"No," Harold chuckled. "She is quite the opposite."

"Can we get down to business now?" Drake asked, not really caring for a lengthy explanation about the male's mate. He was there to talk about Tessa.

"Come on," Harold said, relaxing a bit as he held his hand out for the bear to enter his home.

They walked past the two exam rooms and entered another room at the back of the cottage. Harold's office was small but had a desk and two chairs for patients. His mate was already there, setting the beers on the desk. She excused herself and slipped out of the room, closing the door behind her.

"I'm assuming you've found your mate and she's human?" Harold began.

"Yes, and she wants to be changed, but I can't let her be in pain." Drake lowered his head, pinching the bridge of his nose. "I hear you have some medication I can administer to keep her from hurting."

"I do," Harold replied, and rested his forearms against the top of the desk. "Have you ever changed a human?"

"No," Drake replied, shaking his head.

"The medicine must be administered every four hours," Harold said. "Are you certain you will be of a right mind to take care of your mate during the time when the medicine wears off?"

"I honestly don't know," Drake replied, taking a large swig of cold beer. Could he balance the need to care for her and his beast's agony?

"The change is one of the worst things I've ever seen happen to a human, and I've seen males when they can't take the agony of their mate's distress. Is there anyone who can stand in your place if you have to be sedated alongside her?"

"My brother, Rex, might be able to do it, but he will bring her pain if he touches her," Drake worried. "We've already mated."

"I see," the healer paused and ran a hand over his shaved head, "I can offer my service to you and your mate. I have special gloves I use when I have to care for a mated female. I have assisted in a changing several times, and the gloves keep me from causing them pain."

"Are you sure you want to stay in the heart of bear territory during the change of one of my kind?" Drake asked, being straightforward. The male could be attacked by Drake's bear if the bear was in distress over his mate's pain. If Drake saw Harold touching his mate, even holding her down to give her an injection, the healer could be severely injured.

"I can bring Guardians if you are worried your beast will think of me as a threat," Harold offered.

The healer of the Shaw pride was a good male. His compassion as a doctor and a mated male was not missed.

"I will talk to my mate and set a date," Drake grunted as he climbed to his feet. "As soon as we know, I will call you."

"I will have Guardians on standby," Harold added, taking a drink of his beer.

Chapter 12

A week had passed before Drake had time to sit down with Tessa and talk about the change. He'd been pulling long hours in the fields, planting corn for the season. She'd gone back to work for Tulley, but only a few days a week. She was now off work on the weekends so they could spend time together.

"I don't think I've ever had a weekend off since I started working back in high school." She smiled and sunk down lower into the water in the large Jacuzzi tub in Drake's bathroom. He was leaning against the counter, watching as the bubbles floated around on the top of the water. They were hiding her body from his view, and he wanted to rake them away but he didn't. She needed to relax, and tonight he was going to make sure she was pampered.

"More wine?" he asked, holding up a bottle.

"No," she giggled. "I'm doing fine. Are you going to join me? There's plenty of room."

"Tonight is for you to relax," he said. "You don't want me in there taking up all of your room."

Tessa sat up and took a sip of wine, slipping back into the water as soon as she set the glass on the side of the tub. She stretched her toes above the water, and Drake noticed she'd recently painted them a vibrant red. Her pale leg peeked out as she bent her knee.

"Maybe next time?" she pouted, making him smile wider.

Drake's phone rang from his back pocket, and he grunted when he saw Gunner was calling. It was late, and he'd told his baby brother to leave him and Tessa alone for the night. Whatever he had to say had better be important…more important than spoiling his mate.

"Drake, we've got a trespasser," Gunner cursed across the line.

"Who? Where?" he barked, going on high alert. Tessa sat up so quickly, the water sloshed out of the tub and onto the floor.

"Drake?" she whispered, but he ignored her as his brother spoke.

"Went out front and saw a male body at the tree line toward the road," Gunner panted. Drake could tell he was on foot, and knew it was best to get Tessa locked in the room. He didn't waste time with leaving the bathroom and going to his door to throw the latch.

"Is it human?" Drake demanded. His bear snarled in his head to be set free to search his property.

"It is," Gunner snarled. "Get out here and help me. Rex isn't home."

"I'll lock down the house and be there in just a second. Keep tracking the human," Drake snapped and tucked his phone in his back pocket.

When he turned to get Tessa, she was already standing at the bathroom door, wrapped in a large, brown towel. "What is it, Drake?"

"We have a trespasser," he told her as he reached into his side table drawer to retrieve a gun. "Please tell me you know how to use this?"

"No," she shook her head as her eyes widened, "I've never shot a gun."

"Fuck," Drake swore, taking her hand. He put the revolver against her palm and prayed she'd listen to his quick lesson. "If someone breaks in here, all you have to do is point it in their direction and start pulling the trigger. Understand?"

"Y…yes," she stammered. "Got it."

"I'm locking you inside this room," he stated. "Do *not* come outside until one of us comes for you."

"Drake…" she whimpered, but he silenced her with a kiss.

"Do as you're told, Tessa," Drake said, cupping her face. He wanted her to understand how much she meant to him, and if someone got inside his home and hurt her, he wouldn't be able to survive alone.

"Yes, Sir," she breathed out in a whoosh, and sat heavily on the bed when he released her.

Drake didn't look back as he left the room,

using the key on his keychain to lock the deadbolt. The door was solid and there was no way anyone could get inside unless they had a key or Tessa unlocked the door from the inside.

As soon as he stepped off the front porch, Drake scented the air. His beast rumbled in his mind at the human male who was on his land. The moon shed only a small amount of light across the yard, but Drake shifted his eyes, allowing the animal inside him to partially takeover.

Gunner was about a hundred yards to his left, searching the woods where the human scent lingered. Drake stepped off the porch and stuck close to the side of his house as he made his way toward the trees beside his home.

Once he was able to disappear into the woods, Drake eased up beside his brother. Gunner's eyes were trained on a spot off in the distance. Drake nodded and scanned the area, not seeing or hearing any movement.

"Three o'clock," Gunner whispered so low, his voice was almost silent. Drake took his two fingers and held them up to his eyes before pointing in the direction. Gunner nodded and took Drake's shirt as he slipped it off his body. Within a few seconds, Drake shifted and ambled slowly through the darkness, looking for the trespasser. As soon as his bear latched onto the scent, he followed it west on the property until he reached the fence line. The human had turned north toward the road and that was where the scent faded, blending in with the putrid scent of a vehicle's exhaust.

"He's gone," Drake cursed as he shifted. Gunner's eyes were glowing gold in the darkness.

"Do you think it was Tessa's ex?" Gunner asked, his eyes still trained on the spot in the woods.

"I would almost guarantee it," Drake snarled and pulled his shirt over his head.

Tessa sat in the middle of the bed, her eyes trained on the door, and a gun in her hand. Drake had been gone at least ten minutes, and she was starting to worry about his safety. Who was out there on their land? A hunter?

Her mind already had an idea it could be Bradley. She didn't want him anywhere near the clan, and if she brought trouble to Drake's land, she would be forever sorry. Why couldn't her ex-husband just leave her in peace?

"Tessa, it's Drake!" The sound of his knuckles

tapping on the door caused her to yelp before scrambling off the bed. "I have a key, little one. Put the gun away."

"Come inside, please," she yelled through the door. The gun was still on the bed, and she was waiting for him to step through. Tessa didn't realize how scared she was until she looked down at her shaking hands.

As soon as the door opened, she jumped into his arms. "Are you okay? What happened? Who was it?"

"Woah," Drake said, kissing the top of her head before releasing her to go over to retrieve the gun. He slid it into his side table and turned around to address her. What Tessa saw in his eyes made the shaking turn into full blown tremors.

"Was it him?"

"I don't know." Drake shook his head. His eyes were glowing and his brows were pushed forward. The male she'd given her heart to was angry. No, he was beyond angry. The sharp fangs poking into his bottom lip were proof of that. "He left in a car parked by the road. I know his scent now, and if it's Bradley, I'll know him before I ever lay eyes on the son of a bitch."

Chapter 13

Three weeks had passed, and the crops were planted. Drake lay in the bed with Tessa resting on his chest. It was the first time he'd slept past four in the morning since the winter, and with his mate next to him, he had no reason to move.

Today was the day the panther's healer would change Tessa. She'd tossed and turned the night before, and he knew she was worried. Hell, he was worried, too. By the afternoon, Tessa would be in pain, and Drake would be going out of his mind.

"When will he be here?" Tessa asked as her eyes fluttered open. Drake rolled to his side and cupped her face. This would be the last time he looked into her beautiful sapphire eyes. In three days, they'd be brown.

"At noon," Drake answered. "I want to feed you and bathe you before he gets here. If there are any other questions, I need you to ask them now."

Tessa nuzzled into his chest and took a deep breath. "I want to be able to protect myself, and I want to be with you, Drake."

"You are already mine, Tessa," he reminded her, lifting her chin to kiss her softly.

"I love you, Drake," she said as she smiled at him. "I just want you to know that before I go through the change. I want you to remember that I was a human when I fell in love with you, and it's not because I'll be like you in a few days."

Drake's lips crashed down on hers as the words sank into his stubborn mind. She did love him. "I love you, Tessa Ward, and as soon as you are on your feet, I want you to be my bride. You will never be called by that motherfucker's last name ever again."

"Well, bear man, are you asking me to marry you?" she flirted.

"Will you?" he pressed, waiting for her reply.

"Of course, I will," she winked. "Will you make love to me now, Sir?"

"I'm going to worship your body," he snarled and rolled over to grab a satin sash in his nightstand. "Hands above your head, Tessa."

Tessa didn't hesitate and lifted her arms. She tangled her fingers in the metal headboard and giggled when he wrapped the sash around her wrists, tying it off to one of the horizontal bars of his headboard. Her little sighs of delight hardened his cock to the point of pain, and he ached to be inside her, but she liked the delayed release he so often teased her with. Drake was a man of patience when it came to his mate. He'd give her what they both wanted and prepare her for the next few days.

The clock on the wall read it was nearing ten in the morning. He couldn't spend hours in bed with her, but he had a good idea of how he was going to satisfy his mate. "Close your eyes, Tessa. If you open them, I will stop. Keep them closed, and I will make it worth it."

"Yes, Sir," she breathed.

Drake grasped her tiny shorts at the sides and pulled them free of her body. Her tank top was still on, and he wasn't going to remove it. The sensation of darkness and being half dressed would play with her desire. He wanted her to focus on where their bodies connected.

"Knees up and drop them out to the side," he ordered, waiting while she got into position. Her pussy gleamed with her desire. The scent of honeysuckle was stronger when she was aroused, and he wasn't going to complain.

Without any warning, Drake leaned forward and used his tongue to lap at her intimate flesh. Tessa sucked in a breath, but never opened her eyes. The inside of her thighs quivered with each pass of his tongue. This female was perfect for him. She called to his dominant side, and she loved him for who he was, no matter how much he had tried to push her away that first night on his land.

Tessa's head thrashed from side to side as he took her swollen clit between his teeth, sucking and biting until she almost opened her eyes. When her hips started to rock, he sat back and watched as a pronounced pout formed on her lips.

"Do you want my cock, mate?" he teased, using the back of his finger to trace over her pussy. He blew on her clit and waited for her reply. He smiled as her teeth gritted from the need to come.

"Please, Sir?" she begged.

"Can you hold out a little longer for me, little one?" he asked, dipping his head for another taste.

"I'm trying, Sir," she groaned.

"Good girl," he praised, using his middle finger to slide into her pussy. The moment he was inside, her body tightened, holding him in place. He waited a moment for her to relax before he started the motions.

She didn't gasp out in shock when he kissed her. Tessa opened her mouth and kissed him back, their tongues dueling faster and faster as her need began to rise. He loved watching her shatter beneath him, and he craved her sweet release.

They played this game for another fifteen minutes; the closer she came to orgasm, the more he would stop and blow across her clit. By the time his bear and cock were demanding he mount his mate, Drake was lightheaded from the desire he had for her.

"I'm going to fuck you now, Tessa," he warned as he pushed his shorts down to his knees and climbed between her silky legs. He fisted his cock and brought it to her opening. "I'm going to fuck you hard, and I want you to come now."

"Please, Sir?"

He worked himself deep, stopping only when he was fully seated inside her. He pulled back slowly, testing her body. He leaned over her and wrapped a hand around her throat, sliding it up to hold her face still. "You can look at me now. I want you to remain still while I bring you pleasure."

Tessa's blue eyes locked with his, and she didn't mumble a word as he began to move. The only sound in the room was their bodies slapping together as he pumped into her. Tessa kept her legs out to the side, forever submissive to his wishes.

"Come for me," he said, using his free hand to reach between their bodies. He rolled his thumb over her clit as his cock slammed into her body.

"Yes!" she screamed out in pleasure.

Drake's world was complete. This woman was his, and after he fed her his blood, she'd truly be his forever mate.

Drake eased his cock from Tessa's body as he curled his large frame around her. Today was the day she'd be changed into what he was, and she was ready, no matter hour nervous she was from the thought of being in pain.

The panther's doctor would assist and make sure she was sedated, but there was always a chance she would feel the excruciating pain everyone had warned her about. Three days…she could do that, right? If the medicine worked enough to ease her pain, she could do it. At least, that was what she kept telling herself.

"I'm going to do my best to not leave your side," Drake promised, stroking the hair back from her face.

"I'm going to be okay," she stated, more for his ears than her own. She didn't want him to be upset because he sensed her pain. "If you have to leave me alone, I will understand."

"My brothers and Harold will be there with you," he promised. "Let's get you in the bath, and then I'll feed you. He will be here within the hour."

Tessa nodded and slipped from the bed. Drake followed her and began running water in the large tub. She entered the large walk-in closet where all of her clothes now hung; Drake's on the left and hers on the right. She chose a tank top and a pair of workout shorts.

"So, when I wake up, I'll be a bear?" she asked, needing conformation.

"Yes, the final part of the change is when you shift. I will be with you by that time. My brothers will make sure of it."

"What do I do when I wake up like that?" she frowned.

"You have to get your footing like a newborn would," he tried to explain. "Just be calm and let the beast inside you learn its balance."

"How do I change back?"

"You have to use your mind to command the bear to allow your human side to come forth. Sometimes it's easy, other times, the bear will want to roam. With this first shift, you decide when you want to come back as a human."

"Sounds easy," she groaned, rolling her eyes. "I'm trusting you to not let me eat anyone I'm not supposed to eat."

Drake's head fell back as he laughed. Tessa watched as he checked the temperature of the water, turning to look at her with so much love in his eyes. "I won't let you hurt anyone."

She stepped into the water once he deemed it perfect. The bubbles tickled her neck as she settled in and got comfortable. "Let me bathe you, my mate."

Tessa didn't argue, letting him search for her foot under the water. He lathered up a cloth and got to work. She was floating in bliss as he pampered her. From what he'd said in the beginning about spoiling his mate, Tessa was sure the rest of her life would be like this moment.

"Head back, little one," he ordered softly. "I need to wash your hair."

By the time Drake was done, she was relaxed and limp. If the water was still warm, she wouldn't have gotten out. The clock was nearing noon, and she knew it was almost time. Changing into her comfy clothes, Tessa followed Drake to the main part of the house where he sat her down and fed her a small meal.

"You'll need food for energy, but the doc said you don't want much on your stomach," he said, setting a grilled chicken salad in front of her. He opted for some leftover stew, and they ate in peace until Drake's head lifted from his bowl. His eyes fell on hers and she knew what was happening.

"The healer is here," he announced.

"Okay." She nodded and pushed away her plate. "I'll clean up while you let him inside."

"It's going to be okay," he promised as he pulled her up from the seat. Drake's eyes roamed her face, looking for any fear. She held it back, because she was sure if he scented fear coming from her, he wouldn't change her. No matter how bad he wanted her to be like him, Tessa knew he feared her pain more than anything else.

Tessa quickly scraped the remaining food off the plates and put them in the dishwasher. When she turned around, the healer was just entering the living room with a black bag in his left hand.

"Tessa," he greeted, nodding in her direction.

"Healer," she said as she returned the greeting, using his given profession in the shifter world.

"Are we ready to do this?" he asked, looking over his shoulder to where Drake was waiting. Drake nodded and the healer turned to look at her. She swallowed hard and nodded, dropping a towel on the counter that she was using to dry her hands. "I will wait here until I am of need. You already know what needs to be done."

They did. Harold had come by two weeks ago and explained how the change worked. Drake would need to bite into his own wrist and Tessa would need to drink as much blood as she could until the pain began….and then she'd need to drink more. The healer insisted Drake force the blood down her throat when she cried out from the first bouts of pain. If he didn't, it wouldn't work. He was only allowed to stop when she was too far gone to accept blood.

Drake silently took her hand and led her back to the bedroom, where he closed the door. Tessa pulled all of the blankets off the bed, leaving the fitted sheet and two pillows. When she turned around, Drake was texting his brothers.

"They're meeting with the healer now," he offered. "Are you ready?"

"I'm ready to be yours, Drake."

Drake helped her onto the bed. Tessa sat cross-legged and waited for Drake to join her. He closed his eyes for a moment as if he were praying. The man she loved climbed next to her and cupped her face. He didn't speak before his lips crashed down on hers. The kiss was full of worry and love. When he pulled back, Drake lifted his wrist to his lips. The sound of flesh tearing was the only sound in the room. His eyes flashed gold as he whispered, "Drink."

Tessa didn't have a chance to breathe before he grasped the back of her head and pressed his wrist to her mouth. The coppery taste of his blood flowed over her tongue. She swallowed once, twice, and on the third gulp, a pain twisted her stomach.

"Drink more, Tessa," he growled when she tried to pull away. She could feel the blood as it trickled out the corner of her lips and made a trail down her chin.

"Hurts," she cried, wrapping her hands around his wrists. She wanted to push him away, but she remembered she had to drink. Maybe she shouldn't have done this? Maybe it was going to be too much?

Maybe it was too late?

She drank and sucked at his wrist, needing to

consume as much blood as she could to make the change work. The pains spread from her stomach to her sides. It felt like a million swords were impaled in her body. *Oh, God! Help me!*

"God damn it, Tessa! Drink!" Drake snarled, his fangs descending in a rush. Her eyes locked onto them, and she felt the stirrings of something inside her. The blood began to heat up in her body, and when her body seized, a blood curdling scream bubbled from somewhere deep in her soul.

Chapter 14

Her screams were making his beast prowl in his mind, pushing at his skin to be set free. The scent of his own blood in the air brought the healer to his bedroom door. He had to tamp down his need to protect Tessa and let the male inside.

"I will examine her and give her a sedative," Harold stated as he pulled on a pair of black gloves. They were supposed to keep Tessa from being hurt by the touch of another male. At this point, Drake wouldn't know the difference if the gloves didn't work. Her pain was just too much.

Harold removed a vial and a syringe, filling the needle halfway with medication, and walked over to the bed. Drake held her tightly, trying his hardest to keep her from thrashing around the bed too much. He didn't want her to fall off or hurt herself during the change.

"Roll her toward me so I can access her hip, please," Harold ordered. Drake did as he was told and watched as the healer moved her shorts out of the way, exposing the top of her hip. The injection was quick, and his mate didn't even flinch or try to bat away the healer's hand.

"Thank you," Drake said, gritting his teeth as Tessa continued to squirm and cry from the pain.

"Give the meds about five to ten minutes to work," Harold urged as he disposed of the needle. "I'll be in your living quarters if you need me."

Drake nodded and watched as Harold left the room. The male closed the door and left them alone. He wouldn't be far, taking up residency in Drake's personal living space on the other side of the door.

Tessa's screams were quieting, and Drake was thankful she wasn't in pain. The medicine was working enough to calm her to nothing more than some deep panting. His bear relaxed in his mind, and he wondered if maybe he would be able to go through this without loosing his fucking mind.

He'd never seen a human changed, but had heard of it being done. It wasn't a common occurrence in the shifter world. Before they had been found out by the humans, shifters mostly kept to themselves. Occasionally, one would find their mate in a human and a change would occur if they were destined to be mates. Sometimes, changing a human was necessary in keeping them alive. He knew a few of those cats had changed their human mates over the past few years.

"If you can hear me, little one, I am here with you," Drake whispered as he leaned down to kiss her forehead. She was hot, but shivering. He moved from the bed to gather a thin sheet to lay over her body. She didn't try to kick it away.

The next two hours, he laid with her, petting her as the blood he had given her worked throughout her body. She never cried out, but Drake knew she was still in some pain by the expressions on her face. Her lips were drawn into a thin line and her eyes were squeezed as tightly shut as she could make them.

Drake checked her over, lifting her eyelid to see if there were any changes, and frowned when there were none. It was going to be a long three days, waiting for his mate to come back to him.

He wanted to marry her by human customs. It was imperative she become a Morgan. Some shifters didn't abide by those traditions, living as mated couples without the legal documentation. Many months ago, Drake would've been okay with the same thing, but since meeting Tessa and knowing about her past, he wanted to make that female his in every way possible.

Getting rid of that motherfucker's last name would be the next order of business. Drake was okay with going directly to the court house as soon as she woke up, but he wondered if she wanted a real wedding. The thought of all the frilly attachments that came along with that kind of ceremony gave him a case of the hives.

A scream bubbled out of her throat and Drake

immediately reached for her, calling out for the healer. Her hold on his arm was painful, and he took that as a good sign; the blood was working.

"It's going to be another hour before I can give her more medicine," Harold frowned. "Do I need to get your brothers? Because this is about to get bad until I can inject her again."

"No," he barked. "I'm going to be fine." He knew what he'd said was a lie. As Tessa thrashed on the bed, he felt his beast's agitation boiling beneath his skin. With the next scream, his fangs burst through his gums and he roared at the healer, warning him away from his mate.

The more she screamed, the more Drake's beast pushed for release.

Harold held his hands out in front of him and backed out the door. Within minutes, his brothers entered the room, and that was when all hell broke loose.

Tessa opened her mouth to scream and blood poured out, cutting off her oxygen.

"Healer!" all three men yelled.

The healer entered the room with his bag and pulled on his special gloves. Drake's heart beat a million miles and hour as he held her tight, blood dripping onto his arms. "I can't let her go. What's going on?"

"Her body is rejecting your blood, Drake,"

Harold said, turning her head to the side as she vomited. Rex and Gunner ran to the bathroom and grabbed every clean towel they could find.

"What the fuck are you talking about?" Drake snarled.

"Move!" the healer said, removing some tubing from his bag. He quickly started an IV line in Tessa's arm as Drake held her still. "Give me your arm."

"Why?" Drake paused as the doc came forward with his own needle.

"I need your god damn blood, Drake," Harold snarled. "I have to replace what she threw up, and I'm going to draw it from your arm to put in hers."

"Do whatever you have to do," Drake said, realizing what the healer was saying. He would do anything for her, even if that meant giving Tessa every drop of blood in his body.

"What will happen if you don't give her enough blood?" Rex asked, his brother's eyes watching over Tessa like a doting brother. It was then he realized his brothers considered her family.

"She will be in pain for nothing," Harold said, uncapping the needle with his teeth. He wrapped the band around Drake's upper arm and punctured the vein to insert his own line, using a needle to draw a large amount from the vein, immediately turning toward Tessa to inject it into the line in the crook of her arm.

"Take as much of my blood as you need," Drake panicked, seeing his brothers move closer.

The stick of the needle wasn't painful. There was nothing more painful than watching Tessa suffer. As soon as the doc drew his blood, Drake immediately took Tessa back into his arms, throwing his leg over hers to keep her still.

The moment he injected her with Drake's blood, everything changed. No matter how tight his hold was on his mate, her strength tripled and she convulsed, her back arching at an odd angle. Drake's human side knew it was from the change, but his beast didn't accept it. No, his beast pushed at his skin and his face began to change, his anger and distress taking over.

"Get away!" he snarled around his thick fangs. His fingers had shifted to claws, and the shirt he wore ripped at the seams as his arms began to grow. The shift was upon him, and at this point, there was no turning back.

Hands grabbed at him as he turned on the bed, coming to his feet and crouching down in a protective stance in front of Tessa. His brothers and the healer were moving closer. "I will kill you if you touch her!"

Gunner made a leap, taking him to the ground. Rex sat on his legs as the healer came forward with another needle. He felt the prick to his arm as they held him in place. He tried to fight them, but it was no use. The last thing he remembered was hearing his own agonizing wail.

"Nooooooo!"

Rex sat on the couch in Drake's living quarters, watching as his older brother slept off the sedation. It'd been two days, and Drake had gotten to the point where he couldn't handle it any time Tessa would scream. He hated seeing his brother and sister-in-law hurting so much. He hoped he never had to see another human changed into what they were.

The doc was sleeping on a cot Gunner had pulled into the bedroom. At this point, the healer was Tessa's only caretaker. Gunner and Rex wouldn't be able to touch her even with the special gloves the doc used. Harold was a pro at being careful with a mated female. Even with the gloves, there was a chance Rex or Gunner would slip up and touch her with their forearm while she thrashed. Harold knew what he was doing, and they had to trust him to keep her sedated and unharmed.

The door to Drake's living area opened in a

rush. Gunner stood there with glowing eyes, and Rex knew immediately there was something wrong.

"What is it?" he asked, jumping to his feet.

"Did you hear the fucking shotgun go off out front?" Gunner barked.

"No," Rex snarled. Granted, the room was underground, but his heightened hearing should've detected something as loud as a gunshot.

"That motherfucker is outside, and he's demanding we return his wife!"

"Oh, hell no!" Rex snapped.

"Get his ass up," Gunner ordered, looking over his shoulder. "We have a human to kill."

Rex hurried over to Drake, shaking him as hard as he could. "Man, you gotta wake the fuck up!"

Like a jolt of lightning had struck his big brother, Drake roared as he came to his feet, "Tessa!"

"Not quite, big guy," Rex said, steading Drake. The sedative was still in his system, and his eyes were glassy. "Bradley is on our land. He's shooting at the house and demanding we give him Tessa."

"He's dead!" Drake promised, and stumbled to the bedroom door. He pushed it open, waking the healer. "We have a problem."

"What is it?" Harold asked as he stood from his makeshift bed.

"Her ex is here, and I'm going to go kill him," Drake stated. "Do not leave this room."

"Take care of him, and I'll take care of your mate," Harold promised, touching his fist to his heart in a gesture of pride. The male was a good one. He would be repaid somehow in the future by the Morgan clan. It was guaranteed for protecting a mate.

Tessa didn't know how long she'd been screaming in pain. Time was endless in her mind. It could've been two hours or three days, but something had changed in the last hour. The sounds of her panting changed into a deeper sounding growl. A roar sounded in her head. Her mind felt like it was being pulled in two different directions. Something was pushing at her mind, her skin, her soul.

She could open her eyes now, but not for long. Every time she would wake, the healer would be there to reassure her everything was going according to plan, but Drake was nowhere to be found.

Was he sedated?

Was he going insane like he had mentioned?

"*Drake*," she moaned, feeling something in her mouth. She used her parched tongue to roll across her teeth, sucking in a gasp of air when sharp fangs pricked the tip of her tongue. She was changing into a bear.

"He will be here shortly," the healer reassured her, sitting on the edge of the bed. "You are beginning your shift. Don't fight it, Tessa."

Her fingers tingled as the bones broke and reformed. She screamed out in pain when her back arched at a weird angle. The beast inside her mind wanted out. It needed to hunt, to scavenge the land.

Her beast was hungry.

Tessa remembered Drake telling her not to fight the first shift. The healer had advised her giving in to the beast would make the shift less painful. *Please shift quickly, lady bear.*

The beast controlled her mind and her body as it pushed to be released. Hair sprouted through her human skin, her ears reshaping along with her face. Claws grew from her fingertips and her legs and arms thickened.

The bed cracked and creaked as she blinked. The room around her was covered in a golden haze. The healer stood in the corner, his eyes narrowing on her. "Tessa? You are a beautiful grizzly."

The beast wanted her mate. Where was he?

Tessa roared at the male, wanting answers, but her human mind knew he didn't understand her. They couldn't talk in this form, and who knew if the panther understood bear mannerisms enough to sense what she was wanting.

Tessa slowly crawled off the bed, walking over to the door. Her legs wobbled with each step, but it didn't take but a few to get her balance. The bear lifted its paw and tapped it against the door. She looked over her shoulder and leaned her head toward the exit. The healer sighed heavily and shook his head. "Drake wants you in here."

Another roar.

"Tessa, you have to stay in here," Harold repeated. "The men are taking care of a problem on the land."

Problem? Her human mind and her beast knew something was wrong. The only person who'd come onto this land was Bradley. *Oh no!*

Tessa's beast stood on her hind legs and bashed her large paws against the door, demanding to be set free. Harold cursed loudly behind her but didn't make a move from his spot in the corner. It didn't matter, because with each hit to the door, the wood split little by little.

"Tessa, no!" Harold yelled as the door splintered from the weight of her body slamming against it.

She let the beast run toward the front room. When she came into the large living room, the bear lifted its snout to the sky and scented the air. Drake's scent was strong, along with others she hoped were his brothers.

"Tessa, damn it!" Harold barked as he slid to a stop behind her. "Your ex-husband is out there. You cannot let him see you or the bear."

Drake is out there!

It didn't matter. She was going to kill Bradley now that she had the beast inside her, and the beast wanted that male's blood for coming on their lands. The fact that her mate was out there just sealed the deal. She was going out to confront him. She wanted to see the look on Bradley's face when he came face to face with a grizzly bear.

I hope he pisses himself.

She didn't know how to shift back to her human form to tell Harold to open the door, because she didn't want to destroy another one. As she prowled toward the front of the house, Harold cursed but came around her to stand in front of the door. The bear didn't want to hurt him, but she would take a swipe at him if he didn't move.

"I'll let you out, but don't you fucking get hurt," he snarled, then opened the door.

The moment the door opened, Tessa's bear scented her mate. A gunshot rang off to her left, just inside the woods, and she took off at a dead run.

As she rounded the side of the house, she saw Drake drop to his knees as he held his chest. She could see his eyes glowing from fifty yards away. Tessa's heart shattered at the sight, and her bear roared as it ran faster, panting and tasting Bradley's blood on its tongue.

When Bradley came into view, Tessa's human side gritted her teeth. She wanted to rip him to shreds. Her true mate was on the ground, bleeding from a shotgun wound. The pain of her change was nothing compared to what she was feeling now.

"Tessa!" Bradley called out. He still didn't see her coming, because he was too focused on Drake's body as it lay on the ground. "Where are you?"

Right here, motherfucker!

Bradley's head turned to the left, his eyes going wide as saucers. Her eyes were locked on his as he realized a bear was coming for him at full speed. Out of the corner of her eye, she saw movement, but didn't look to see who, or what, it was. All she wanted was Bradley's life.

A roar split the night as a flash of brown filled the space between Tessa and Bradley. The scent of blood in the air doubled as Drake's bear landed on Bradley, taking him to the ground by the throat.

"Tessa! Get out of here!" Rex yelled from behind her. She looked over her shoulder and saw the two brothers running for them. Gunner was already throwing his clothes off as he began to shift. Within seconds, another bear ran past her, stopping a few feet from Drake. "Come on, Tessa. This is Drake's right as your mate."

She wanted to scream at them. She wanted to push Drake out of the way. He'd been shot!

"He's fine," Rex promised, and stood in front of her. "You don't want to see this. Go inside."

Her beast panted and small growls sounded from somewhere deep inside the bear. Drake was hers, and she'd be damned if he took Bradley out without her there.

With one swipe of her paw, she pushed Rex out of the way. He yelled for her to stop, but she took off at a dead run, ducking her head to push Drake off of her ex-husband. It took one look at her to make Bradley scream out in fear.

His throat was already bleeding, the scent was like ambrosia on the air. The man lying on the ground had tormented her for years. Seeing him in the same position she'd been in several times was the biggest gift karma could've ever delivered.

"Tessa!" Drake's human voice echoed off the trees. Her name was a command in the air, and she looked up at him as he marched toward them. He was stark naked, covered in sweat, and his eyes still glowed with the anger of his beast. "Kill him, or I will."

"Yeah, you stupid bitch, kill me," Bradley snarled from the ground as he held his throat. Blood seeped through his fingers, assuring Drake had already broken his prey's skin. "So, you're a fucking shifter? Ha! You're better off with these idiots. Maybe they can get some use out of you."

"You son of a bitch!" Drake roared as he shifted again, pushing Tessa away as her true mate took him by the throat again.

The sound of Bradley's air leaving his body was softer, less morbid than it should've been when Drake ripped out his throat with his fangs. Tessa's bear backed away when Drake's bear turned for her. He had blood all over his snout, but it didn't seem to bother him. He just prowled toward her as if she was his next victim.

Please, let me be a human.

The thought was followed by a tingling in her spine. Tessa's bear eased itself to the ground, resting on its belly, and the shift began, returning her to her human self. The bear in her mind slinked away and quieted, content with the kill her mate had made to protect her.

"Drake?" she whispered as soon as her human voice returned. She didn't care that she was naked. She didn't care that Rex and Gunner were watching them. The only thing Tessa wanted was for Drake to shift to his human body and take her away from Bradley. "It's over. It's over. It's over."

Tessa covered her face with her hands as the

tears fell from her eyes. Bradley was dead and she was free. She was finally free from running and worrying for her life. Warm hands wrapped around her body and lifted her from the ground. She knew immediately it was Drake, but she didn't uncover her face. There was no need. Her new senses could tell it was him.

"Shh, I've got you," he whispered against her hair.

Chapter 15

May

Tessa woke from a dream about the bouquet of various blue flowers Drake had brought home the night before, smiling into the darkness of their bedroom as she brought up the image of the night before in her mind's eye. He looked awkward walking into the house with the plastic-wrapped bouquet in his large hand, but she didn't make fun of him. No, she loved the sentiment so much, she'd made him skip dinner and took him to bed.

They spent the evening curled up together after a marathon round of sex. Drake was a demanding lover, and she was happy to let him take the lead. There was nothing she wanted more than a man who could dominate her in the bedroom, but not control her life. She'd had enough of that with Bradley.

She shook her head to clear her thoughts of her former life. Bradley would not hold anymore space in her mind. Drake completed her in so many ways. Who knew she'd find the man she was destined to love and change her species all within a month of each other?

Some days, Tessa still couldn't believe she could shift into a bear. She had a strength about her she'd only seen in super hero movies. Only this was real life.

Reaching for the other side of the bed, she sighed when she found a cool spot where Drake slept. He probably woke up before dawn to check on his fields. Rex and Gunner would be with him, and she could get some payments made for the business.

Tessa had quit the diner and Tulley's parts shop a few weeks ago after Drake convinced her to work for him. She made a nice wage, and she was sure he paid her more than her worth, but he said he had always hated the paperwork part of the business. After she'd gotten a gander at his inbox, she immediately made her decision to help him at home.

The clock on the bedside table said it was nearing eight in the morning when she finally climbed out of bed, grabbing clothes as she headed for the shower. She did nothing more than wash and dry her hair, pulling it up into a sloppy bun at the top of her head. Drake told her she was beautiful without makeup, but she wore it anyway. Today would be no different.

The scent of coffee tickled her nose when she entered the main house, and she found her favorite cup sitting by the pot, a spoon resting inside. Tessa smiled at the gesture and made her coffee.

Right before she took the first sip, her phone rang, and her mother's number flashed across the screen. A smile as bright as a million suns lit up her face as she answered, "Hey momma!"

"Tessa girl, how are you?" her mother said into the phone.

"I'm so happy, mama," Tessa replied, setting her cup beside the computer's keyboard. "When will you be here?"

"Our plane lands at two tomorrow afternoon," she stated. "Your brother is threatening your fiancé's life if he is an asshole."

"Mom!" Tessa gasped. "He's a good man."

"Yeah, well," her mom tsked. "I also told your brother that he better be careful, because those shifters were brutal and would eat him."

Tessa laughed loudly. Her mother knew about Drake. Drake had encouraged Tessa to tell her mom and brother what they were, and how she was also one of them now. Her mom had taken the news as if Tessa had called her to tell her she'd adopted a new puppy. Wait…that wasn't the best analogy. Maybe more like she'd gotten an upgraded apartment.

"Mom, I don't think Drake will eat him," Tessa sighed. "He's anxious to meet you and Ross."

"I'm ready to meet him," she said. Tessa could hear the happiness in her mother's voice. She hadn't heard that in a very long time. Over the past few years, there had been sadness there whenever they would talk.

"He saved my life, momma," Tessa sniffled.

God, she hated crying. She didn't tell her family that Drake had killed Bradley in a fit of rage. Even then, Tessa knew why Drake did it, and she learned later on that shifter law was a lot different from the human ones. Tessa had no remorse for the feelings her newfound species had about the killing, either. In her mind, and the mind of her bear, the kill was justified.

"I know he did, baby girl," her mom replied.

They talked for a few more minutes, and Tessa promised to be at the airport to pick them up the next afternoon. Her mom was going to help her plan a quick wedding with Drake to make it official by human laws.

Drake wanted her to be a Morgan, and she had no problems with changing her name. The moment she fell in love with Drake, Tessa already felt like she was a part of the family. Rex and Gunner had treated her like a sister from the moment they'd met.

Gunner was the sweetest, most accepting of her in the beginning, and Rex took a few days to warm up to her, and she assumed he only did it because Drake had touched her and found out they were true mates.

Realizing her coffee was going cold, she lifted the cup to her lips and took a sip. The moment it hit her stomach, her gut twisted and Tessa shot up from the chair. She ran for the half bath off the kitchen and barely made it in time to retch up the coffee and whatever was in her stomach.

"Tessa!" Drake called out. She tried to kick the door closed, but his large hand caught it before it closed completely. "What's…"

Tessa laid her head sideways on the toilet seat and looked at her mate. His eyes were as wide as saucers, and his hands shook as he moved toward her. "What are you doing?"

Drake dropped to his knees beside her and pulled her body to his. The warmth and feel of him wrapped around her took the nausea away, but only for a moment. She swayed a little as she sat on the floor but didn't throw up again.

"My mate," he sighed and held her close. "You've made me the happiest male on the face of the planet."

"Oh my god, Drake," she moaned. "Why would my throwing up make you so happy?"

"Do you feel different?"

"Of course, I do," she complained. "I'm sick."

"Little one, you're not sick," he cooed, stroking her hair. "You're pregnant."

"W…what?" she gasped. There was no way.

"I can scent your pregnancy," he explained, wonder coating his words. Drake placed his large hand on her flat stomach.

"How? When?" she stuttered. "How the hell can you scent it?"

"You can't?" he frowned, inhaling deep.

"No, I can't!" she barked. "All I've been doing is throwing up since I drank that coffee."

"Oh, no," he shook his head, standing up from his position on the floor. "No more coffee for you. It's bad for my son. Come on, let me take you back to bed."

"Your son?" she asked, her eyes still wide as he scooped her up off the floor.

As soon as Drake's brothers entered the living room, Rex and Gunner froze in their steps and scented the air. Both men whooped loud enough to startle Tess. "Y'all are scaring me."

"Holy shit! We're going to be uncles," Gunner laughed loudly.

"Oh my god," Tessa gasped and covered her face. "You can scent that?"

"Shifters can scent pregnancies within hours after conception," Rex blushed.

"Great, no privacy at all," she mumbled against Drake's shirt. It smelled of dirt and hard work. "Are you sure I'm pregnant?"

"One hundred percent," Drake beamed. Tessa loved when he dropped the grumpy demeanor and showed his happiness. It wasn't very often, but since they'd mated, she was seeing it more and more. "We can always have Harold come over to check you out."

"I'd prefer that," Tessa agreed. "I mean, I trust you guys, but I just need some reassurance."

"I'll get him over this afternoon," Drake promised, pulling out his phone. He composed a quick text and slid it back into his pocket. "For now, you need to rest. I will make you something to eat. Our cub needs strength."

"I'm not going to argue with you on that," she mumbled as she paused to yawn.

Drake's brothers high-fived him as he returned to the main house. He was overjoyed that Tessa had become pregnant after their alone time the night before. Her scent had changed drastically since the night before, and he hadn't noticed when he'd woken up at five in the morning, because he had been in a hurry to get out to the fields.

"You're going to make a great papa, Drake," Rex commented. Drake nodded and looked over his shoulder, knowing Tessa needed to rest, but he wanted to celebrate. "We will have a feast tonight in celebration."

"I'll make something easy on her stomach." Gunner smiled and walked into the kitchen, digging through the freezer for a pack of chicken.

"Thank you both," Drake said, clearing his throat. He felt emotions inside him he'd never felt before. His beast was roaring with its happiness, as well.

"Get your work done, and probably Tessa's too," Rex ordered. "She'll be tired for the next few days."

"I agree," Drake said, wandering off to the computer desk in the living room. He looked around the house and realized he probably needed to add on to the main house. There would be a cub running around soon and having their small office in the living area would cause problems. Maybe he could bust out the wall in front of him and add an actual office with a door?

It wouldn't be any trouble. The cats had a construction company, and he was sure they'd send over a few of their employees to help him.

What the hell was wrong with him? Humans worked for Shaw Construction and he was willingly wanting them to come work on his home. Two months ago, he would've bared his fangs at the thought of a human coming on his land, but now,

Tessa had softened his heart to the other species.

Her mother and brother would be arriving the following day for a small wedding. He'd encouraged Tessa to tell her family about him. He didn't want her to hide from the ones who loved her. Thankfully, her family was as understanding about their secrecy as Tessa had been when she'd found out about them.

His phone pinged with an incoming text. Harold would be out to the house in the next twenty minutes, and Drake figured he'd use that time to pay some bills for the business. After the doc checked Tessa, he'd encourage her to sleep until dinner.

Harold arrived ahead of his schedule, and Rex let the panther's healer inside immediately. Everyone was smiling, and Drake accepted a hearty handshake from the doc. "Congratulations, Drake."

"Thank you!" He smiled, again.

"So, is Tessa okay?" Harold asked as he set his black bag on the kitchen table.

"She's still new to this and wants you to give her a pregnancy test to confirm what we've told her." Drake walked over to the fridge and pulled out a beer, cracking the top even though it was the middle of the day.

"Let's go reassure your mate," Harold chuckled, slapping Drake's back.

He left Harold in his private living area as he slipped inside their bedroom. Tessa wasn't in the bed, and if it wasn't for the light glowing from under the bathroom door, he would've panicked, wondering where she was.

He knocked softly, and after a mumbled response from her, he entered to find her resting her head on the toilet seat. His mate was sick, and he had no idea how to make her better.

"Harold's here," he whispered, and rubbed his hand over her silky, blonde hair. Tessa nodded and started to get up from the floor, but Drake scooped her up and took her back to bed. As soon as she was settled, he stepped out to get the healer.

A quick pregnancy test confirmed their senses, and Harold spent another few minutes checking her vitals.

"I'm so happy," Tessa started crying.

"So am I, little one," Drake cooed as he lay beside her on the bed, looking up at the healer. "Is there anything we can do for this sickness?"

"Bland foods for the next few weeks," Harold stated. "She will need to stay hydrated. If she has any weird symptoms, I'm only a call away."

"So, our baby is okay?" she asked.

"Your cub is going to be strong," Harold promised. "I will be able to check his or her heartbeat in about nine weeks to confirm that for you."

"I can't wait." Tessa smiled at Drake.

"I will leave you and your family to celebrate,"

Harold said, removing his special gloves. Shaking Drake's hand, the healer told them to call him if she had any problems and left the room.

As soon as he left, Drake returned to his mate and pulled her in close. He kissed the top of her head and just kept his lips pressed there for several minutes. "I am the luckiest male alive."

"My mother is going to be so happy," she sniffled. "My brother has never married."

"I can't wait to meet your family," he said, reaching behind him to fluff a pillow. He leaned back and pulled her to his chest. The scent of her pregnancy reached his nose, and he sighed from the peace and calm it brought him.

"Even if they're human?" she asked. Drake looked down and saw a frown form between her eyes.

"They're your family. Of course, I'll love them as you love them."

"Thank you," she grinned, rubbing her hand over his chest. "Thank you for saving me, Drake."

"I think it was you that saved me," he argued.

"How's that?" Tessa sat up so she could look him in the eyes.

"I was so angry that a human took my parents, I turned that into hatred for all humans." He paused to take a deep breath. "You showed me that there are still good humans out there, and you loved me even when I was being a grumpy asshole."

"You really were a grumpy asshole," she confirmed, giggling when he tightened his hold on her.

Epilogue

January

There was snow falling on New Year's Day, and Drake only knew about it when he woke up to check on Tessa. She'd been craving some hot chocolate, and he sleepily made his way to the main house to find some extra supplies.

The Morgan clan had retired to their private rooms to hibernate for the winter about three weeks prior. Drake was beyond tired, because he couldn't rest like he'd done all those winters in the past. His cub was due any day, and his beast wouldn't let him sleep more than a few hours at a time.

Tessa, on the other hand, had been sleeping like a pregnant bear should. He only woke her to check on the babe, and when he did, she'd beg for food. That was normal and nothing to worry about, but it made for a tiring winter rest. After the hot chocolate, Tessa would hopefully sleep another few hours, and Drake could get some rest, finally. He didn't care. As tired as he was, he'd do this every winter if his mate was carrying his cub.

As he descended to his room, he heard Tessa suck in a harsh breath. It took him three steps to push the door open to their quarters. "Tessa?"

"The baby is coming," Tessa panted as he entered the bedroom. She was standing beside the bed, bent over as her hands rested on the tops of her knees. A puddle of water pooled between her feet.

"Okay, little one," he said, setting the cup of hot chocolate on the bedside table. "Let me get the bed prepared. I need you to sit in this chair."

He maneuvered her to the recliner next to their bed. He grabbed a blanket from the end of the bed and set it down before she slowly eased into the seat. Stripping the sheets from the bed, he retrieved a plastic sheet and placed it over the mattress. He'd been planning and training for this day since he came of age many years ago.

"Do we need to call Harold?" she asked. "Are you sure you can do this by yourself?"

Drake smiled where she couldn't see it. Even in labor, his mate was full of questions. He wouldn't change that for anything in the world.

"I know what I'm doing, but if you would like for him to assist me, I can place a call right now," he offered.

"I want you to deliver our cub." She paused, panting as she rested her hand on top of her rounded belly. He checked the clock to keep time of her contractions. "Can you call him though? Can we keep him on standby should anything happen?"

"I can do that," he replied, finishing up what he needed to do so he could focus his time on her comfort. "I'm going to help you back into the bed, and we will wait until the cub is ready to come into the world."

Tessa took his hand after arguing she could do it herself. With a hard glare, Tessa smiled and shook her head, "Yes, Sir."

"Good girl."

He took a moment to text the cat's healer, and a reply came back with an offer to help if he was needed. Drake told Harold he'd be in touch. He climbed into the bed beside Tessa and held her through the next contraction.

Eight minutes apart.

The next few hours were spent with Tessa increasingly becoming more uncomfortable. She cried a few times, but never complained about the pain. Drake was in awe of her strength.

"Have you picked a name?" he asked, trying to keep her mind off of the contractions.

Four minutes apart.

Tessa nodded her head and squinted her eyes when the next contraction hit. She breathed through it, and finally fell back into the pillow. Drake took a cool washcloth and laid it across her forehead.

"I can't believe I have the sole responsibility of giving our child a name." She rolled her eyes, rubbing absently at their child through her belly.

"It's tradition," he shrugged. "I hope you picked my son a strong name."

"I only picked a name for a girl," she teased and sucked in another breath. The contractions were changing, and Drake waited patiently for Tessa to breathe through them.

Three minutes apart.

"Oh, no," he teased, tweaking her nose. "It's going to be a boy."

"It's a girl," she argued, narrowing her eyes.

"You can't know that," he frowned. "Unless Harold told you what the sex of our cub was after that last ultrasound."

Tessa shrugged and laughed, "He didn't tell me. I just *feel* like it's a girl."

"Well, I *feel* it's a boy." Drake knew she was teasing him, and he loved her for it.

"I guess we will find out soon," she winked and cuddled closer to his side. He rested his hand on her belly where his cub still remained within the protection of its mother's womb.

The next contraction hit and Tessa curled in on herself. Drake soothed her by petting her head and whispering encouraging words in her ear. She didn't cry out again, but he could feel her pain as if it was his own.

Two minutes apart.

"I feel pressure," she said a few moments later.

"Let me look," he offered and took his position at the end of the bed. Drake steadied his hand and pushed her gown up where he could see if the cub's head was visible. Tessa cursed when he shook his head. "Not yet, little one."

"I can't do this much longer," she panted with the next contraction.

"It's almost time," he promised.

"I really need to push, Drake," she said, gritting her teeth.

"Not yet, Tessa," he ordered. "You will push when I tell you to."

"It hurts," she cried out when the next contraction hit.

Within fifteen minutes, Tessa was in so much pain, Drake actually became worried. He shot off a text to his brothers and the healer. He hoped Rex and Gunner were awake enough to hear the messages. Harold replied he could be at the house in ten minutes, but Drake held him off. Tessa wanted Drake to bring their cub into the world, and he was going to give her that wish.

"Okay, Tessa, I need you to push on the next contraction," Drake said after taking a look.

The next hour was hectic as Tessa worked her body to deliver their child. Drake stayed focused and did everything exactly the way he was trained.

Finally, at five minutes before midnight, his daughter was delivered. He held the cub close to his heart as he cut the umbilical cord.

"It's a girl," he said in awe. At that moment, he didn't care what sex the cub was, because the child was his and Tessa's.

And she was perfect.

Her face was rounded like a cherub and her legs were long and thick. His thumb slipped into her tiny palm and she squeezed him hard and tight. "Aren't you the strong one?"

"Let me see her," Tessa begged, tears streaming down her face. "Give me my daughter."

Drake carefully bundled his daughter and rested her against Tessa's chest. His mate brought their cub to her breast, and he watched as she fed for the first time. His eyes were wide as he stared at not only one woman he loved with all of his soul, but two women who completely owned him.

"What's her name?" he asked as he kissed Tessa head.

"Her name is Aria Shay Morgan," she announced with a grin, looking up into his eyes.

"It's beautiful."

Drake held his mate and cub, thankful for the day that Tulley sent Tessa to his land. She'd taught him how to love and gave him everything he ever wanted in a mate, and now she had provided him an offspring.

"I love you, little ones," he said to them both as Aria and Tessa dozed off to sleep.

The End…

Keep reading for a look at Talon (Rise of the Pride, Book 1)

Talon (Rise of the Pride, Book 1)
By Theresa Hissong

Chapter One

The footage had been seen on every news outlet around the world. Two men were filmed shifting into black panthers at the edge of a forest in northern Mississippi. The video was as clear as the blue sky above. They'd been seen and the entire world now knew that shifters existed.

Talon Shaw gritted his teeth at the reporter who kept asking some of the most idiotic questions he'd ever heard in his life. Why the fuck they wanted to know about their mating rituals was beyond intrusive, and he sure as hell wasn't going to let that bit of information out into the general public. Every human would run away screaming if they had any idea how mating occurred.

He'd been in talks with local law enforcement and the media for almost a week now. If Ranger and Kye hadn't been so stupid, they wouldn't be in this situation. They'd be living peacefully on the pride's two hundred acre ranch south of town with no one the wiser.

"How long have your kind been around?" a reporter asked.

"Where did you come from?" another chimed in, talking over everyone else.

"Are you dangerous?" a cute blonde asked, raising her hand.

"Our kind have been around for thousands of years," Talon began, looking out into the sea of human reporters. It was hard not to lash out at the reporters for their increasingly impertinent questions. "We are a peaceful group, usually keeping to ourselves. Our ancestors were warriors for kings in ancient times. Panthers have no hatred toward anyone, human or animal."

"How old are you?" a male reporter asked, leaning forward to make himself visible. Talon recognized him from the local station.

"I am twenty nine years old," he answered, catching sight of his younger brother, Noah, standing off to the side. Talon scanned the room and found his second in command, Winter, waiting off to his right. As his eyes moved back across the room, Noah made a sign for Talon to finish answering questions.

"And you are the leader of this…pride?" the male asked, looking confused over his choice of words.

They were different from their animal cousins. Usually, panthers were solitary animals, only coming together to procreate. Since the beginning of time, the shifters had stuck close together, maintaining a family environment. Their ancestors actually coined the name "pride" in reference to their families.

Their animal form wasn't quite like the big cats in the jungles of the world. From a distance, you'd say they were panther, but their genetic makeup was more than just one breed. In fact, their animal bodies were bigger and different from their animal cousins in the wild. They did not have darkened rosettes like some black cats, either. Their genes were not a pigmentation flaw like scientists liked to use in reference to the wild black cats. No, Talon and his pride were just black, panther-like cats that lived in the human world.

"Yes, I am. Every pride has a leader, an alpha. It is his responsibility to nurture and provide for his people. Without the leadership of an alpha, the pride would suffer and eventually die out. It is my responsibility to make sure that they have work and a safe environment to live and raise their young."

"Are there other shifters out there?" the blonde woman asked.

"This is about my pride, and I will only speak about them," he said, his voice holding a warning. It wasn't his place to tell the secrets of the other shifters.

"So, there *are* others?" she pushed, leaning forward. "Are there wolves? Like in the movies? What about other animals?" The woman's eyes took on a dreamy haze and Talon cringed.

"Next question," he responded curtly, looking away from the woman. He hoped like hell that she didn't push him any further to answer those damn questions.

"You own a few companies, Mr. Shaw," another reporter began. "Is this how you provide? Do you only employ your own kind?"

"I employ members of my pride and humans," he said, trying his best not to fidget in his seat. He had to answer these questions as honestly as possible, but not so honestly that the people who worked for him would be targeted.

"Did the humans know that you shift into an animal?" a woman called out.

"No," he answered simply.

He didn't want to scare the humans. The last thing their kind needed was for the humans to hunt them down out of fear. There were many things about shifters that he would take to his grave. There was no way in hell Talon was going to let the humans know that they could be transformed into a shifter with a blood exchange and excruciating pain while the human's body transformed into an animal.

The questions kept coming and eventually his time was up. His brother, Noah, and his second in command, Winter Blue, escorted Talon to an awaiting SUV, whisking him away from the steps of the City

Hall building. The camera flashes caused the panthers to squint, the light irritating their sensitive eyes.

"I'm so glad that's over," Talon sighed, leaning back in his seat. It'd been a long day of answering increasingly personal questions.

"We should be able to breathe a little this weekend." Noah smiled. "I don't know about you, but I'm ready to have a beer."

"That sounds like a great idea," Talon agreed, finally beginning to relax. "Let's hit up *The Deuce* for dinner."

"Do you think there will be a problem?" Winter frowned. Winter was not only his second in command, but also the head of his security company, S.S.S. or Shaw Security Specialists, as the sign over their office complex stated.

"No," Talon replied. "We will not run away from this town. Running only makes them believe that we have something to hide. This pride will continue their daily routines regardless of the media and whatever they say."

"Then a beer it is," Noah cheerfully proclaimed. "Let's hope that little bar owner is there tonight."

"Just a beer, Noah," Talon warned, not giving away any emotions. He didn't want to think about the woman that owned the bar they visited.

Liberty Raines was there most nights, but that didn't mean that they'd interacted with her very often.

There'd been a few times that she'd come by the table to drop off drinks or food. She was always too busy working for them to strike up a conversation. There was something about the little brunette that sent Talon's panther into a growling frenzy. It must've been her scent. Oh, he could pick it out of a crowd. The combination of wildflowers and sunshine was permanently etched into his brain.

The last thing he needed in his life was a woman. He had too many things going on now that they'd been outed by the humans. The fact that she was a human sealed the deal on the certainty that he wanted nothing to do with her. A panther and a human didn't mix, and he sure as hell wasn't going to drag a human into his world.

Not now…not ever.

Talon is available for FREE on Amazon, Kobo, Nook, iBooks, and Smashwords.

About Theresa Hissong:

Theresa Hissong is the bestselling author of the Rise of the Pride series. She writes paranormal romance, rockstar romance, and romantic suspense.

She enjoys spending her days and nights creating the perfect love affair, and she takes those ideas to paper. When she's not writing, Theresa spends her free time traveling and attending concerts all over the United States.

Look for other exciting reads…coming very soon!